Merry in
MOOSE FALLS

Cover Art by Seaj Art

Cover Design by Emily Silver

Editing by Happily Editing Anns

www.authoremilysilver.com

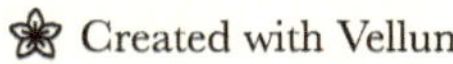 Created with Vellum

MERRY IN MOOSE FALLS

A Moose Falls Novel

EMILY SILVER

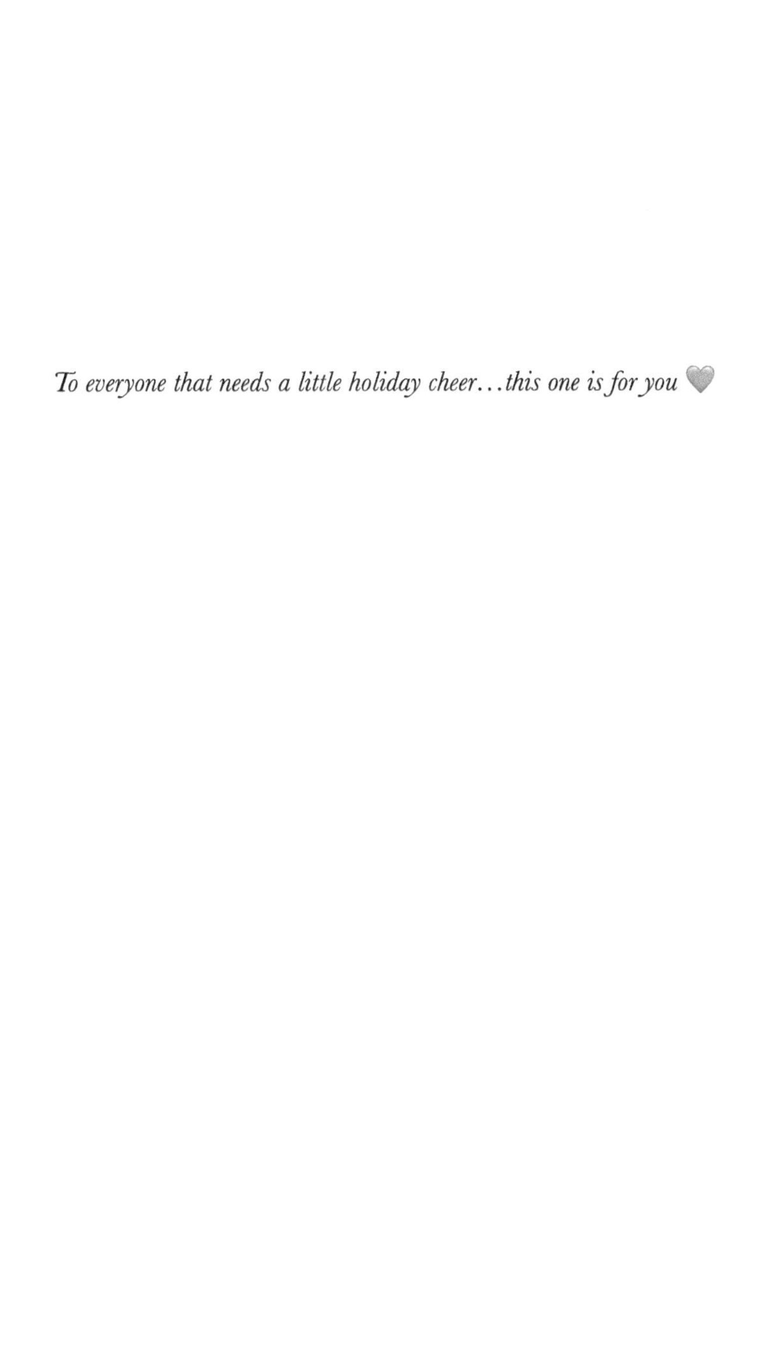

To everyone that needs a little holiday cheer…this one is for you 🤍

THE WORST DAY EVER

Breathe, Charlie. Breathe.

I drag my shirt collar away from my neck, needing relief from the sweltering hell of summer heat. Figures my best friend would get married on the hottest day in Moose Falls, Maine.

The park where they are getting married transformed overnight, it seems. A large, hardwood floor takes up the entire area under the tent. Round tables, with ten chairs seating guests dressed to the nines, have bouquets of extravagant flowers that I couldn't name reaching toward the twinkling lights that hang down. A DJ is playing a lively tune as I sip my drink and watch everyone in front of me from my spot at the head table.

Aside from the heat, it's the perfect day for a wedding. The perfect opportunity to show Brooks how much I support him as he marries the woman he loves.

The perfect day.

Maybe if I keep telling myself that, it will make the sick feeling in the pit of my stomach go away.

It doesn't get any better when the DJ calls everyone's attention to start the speeches.

Breathe, Charlie. Breathe. You can do this.

"You've been my best friend for as long as I can remember, Dee."

I snort around the wine I'm sipping on, getting an elbow to the side from Brooks. Delia and Britney have known each other for two years. Is it really that hard to remember? Brooks and I have known each other since third grade when his family moved to town.

And I've been in love with him since sixth grade when I realized what my feelings meant.

I really need something stronger than wine to get through the rest of this night. I hate how close they're sitting. The way they're touching. The way they move together.

When he told me he was planning on proposing, I congratulated him and then went home to cry. I knew I'd never have him, but it didn't make the pain any easier.

If only I could find someone. Maybe that would help ease the sting I'm feeling as I force myself to sit still and listen to the maid of honor wax poetically about how Delia knew Brooks was the one.

I recall him saying something like this to me when he first told me about her. *When you know, you know.* I know the feeling. It hit me when I knew Brooks was the one for me.

Clapping brings me back to reality. Being in love with your straight best friend? The worst.

"Now let's hear from the best man, Charlie Palmer."

Gulping down the rest of my wine, I grab the mic from Britney and stand.

Breathe, Charlie, breathe.

Delia's arm is wrapped around Brooks, her thumb stroking his shoulder. I shouldn't notice these things, but I do.

I hate that I do.

I clear my throat and glance down at my best friend who is staring up at me with a huge smile on his face. Turning to face the crowd, I start the speech I've had written for weeks.

"I've known Brooks since he moved to town in third grade. Our teacher asked me to show him around school, and we've been friends ever since. The awkward middle school years…"

"God, those were the worst!" Brooks laughs, everyone joining in.

"I think it was easier for you than me. At least it got easier for me in high school. I always had you at my side. Trying out for the soccer team and failing. Stuttering my way through speech team. Wherever I was, there you were. We were inseparable. The best times of my life always involved you."

He's grinning up at me, pride and love shining in his hazel eyes. They're framed by the expert coif of his auburn hair, and my stomach clenches as I realize I prefer the shaggy mess of his hair to this perfect look today.

Not love for me, mind you. I've dreamed of those eyes looking at me like that for years. But it will never happen. I have to push down the feelings I have for Brooks and finish this speech.

I can get drunk and wallow in my feelings after.

"And then we went off to college. Brooks came home that first Thanksgiving and couldn't stop talking about the girl he met. About how much he loved her and wanted to marry her."

They're both smiling at each other now. That dopey, cheesy face of two people who just got married.

The pang in my gut grows deeper. I wish it would swallow me whole.

"Everything was all about Delia. I think I could have told anyone in town Delia's life story after that break." I laugh. "I saw the way his face lit up talking about this person. From that moment, I knew she would be a special person in his life. Brooks had never talked about anyone like that."

Like me. I clear my throat, taking a sip of wine from a new glass that was just dropped off by a passing waiter before continuing.

"If you've been around Brooks and Delia at all, you know this is true love. They've had some hard times together, but it's made them stronger. Cemented the bond the two of them have. Their love is the kind of love we all hope to find."

Grabbing what's left of my wine, I hold up my glass.

"Please join me in toasting Brooks and Delia. To a love that they deserve and we all hope to have one day."

"To Brooks and Delia!" the crowd echoes around me as the two of them kiss.

I'm done. All my best man duties are *finally* done. I can drown my sorrows in the good stuff at the bar and then start the hard work tomorrow. The hard work of trying not to be in love with my best friend.

Brooks stands, pulling me into his strong arms. "I love you, Charlie. Thank you for standing by my side today. You're my best friend."

"There's nowhere else I'd be. I love you, Brooks."

I hate the way my entire body tenses along with the goose bumps that break out on my skin despite the heat. If only he loved me the way I love him.

Being in love with your best friend is the worst.

Chapter One

A DECEMBER TO FORGET

"Who divorces someone in December?" I bemoan into my almost empty drink.

"Technically it was finalized in December," Charlie oh-so-helpfully points out.

I cut my best friend a scathing glare.

"What? I said technically," Charlie says.

"It doesn't change the fact that I'm divorced and it's December. Who does that before the holidays?" I point a finger at him. "And don't hit me with your technicalities."

Charlie throws his hands up. "I wasn't going to."

"I need another drink."

"Got it."

Charlie pops up from his spot across from me at the table to dash behind the bar. I guess this is one of the perks of being best friends with someone who owns a bar.

The Tinsel Tavern is quiet given it is an early weekday

afternoon. Canned lights and twinkling string lights brighten the large room. A few patrons are sitting at tables drinking mixed cocktails. The usually crowded dance floor is empty. Old Pride posters hang on the wall, next to photos of the various drinks served and old pictures of what the Tinsel Tavern used to look like.

This place has become like a second home. With Charlie owning it, he spends most of his time here. If I want to hang out with him, this is where I come.

"Two shots of tequila."

Charlie sets two small glasses of amber liquid in front of me. Not thinking, I down both in under ten seconds. It burns going down, but it helps calm the rage I'm currently feeling.

"Fuck." I grab the glass of water Charlie brought over earlier when I told him I needed to get drunk and take a healthy swallow. "I'm going to need about ten more of those."

Charlie smiles at me, sipping on his beer. "You're going to need to drink about ten more glasses of water if you think I'm going to keep feeding you shots."

"Please?" I whine, jutting out my bottom lip before dropping my arms onto the table and resting my head there. "I'm sad."

"I thought you were angry?" Charlie rests his arm on the back of the corner booth we're sitting in. This is Charlie's booth. Whenever his friends come hang out, this is our spot.

"Again, with the technicalities. I'm sad too. I can be both."

"Who's sad about what?" a voice interrupts the conversation.

Glancing up, I find one of Charlie's other good friends standing at the end of the table. Hunter is tall, with biceps that are thick under his jacket. Blond hair is hidden below a dark, knit cap, and his blue eyes don't give away anything.

Hunter moved to Moose Falls a few years back and became fast friends with Charlie. For as much as I've hung out with him, it's hard to get a read on him.

"My divorce," I lament.

"Ouch." Hunter drops down into the open seat next to Charlie. "Sorry, man."

"I guess it was time." I gulp more water before flagging down a passing waiter to order more shots.

"Still." Hunter reaches across the table and claps me on the shoulder. "That has to hurt."

"It'll be okay," Charlie tells me, putting a positive spin on it. Which is just like him. "Lick your wounds, heal from this, and then I'm sure you'll meet someone new and fall madly in love and get married again."

I scoff. "I will never get married again, even if the world is on fire and it would save humanity."

Charlie chokes on his sip of beer. "That's quite the stance to take."

"Well, it's true."

A few minutes later, the waiter drops off the shots I ordered and I pass one to each of the guys. "Cheers to life being over."

"I don't know how I feel about that, but I'll drink." Hunter clinks his glass against mine before downing his shot. Charlie rolls his eyes at me but follows suit.

"You really should slow down," Charlie tells me. "You'll only feel more terrible in the morning if you keep going."

Hunter laughs. "*Or* you could take a page out of Charlie's playbook and get drunk in Canada."

"I'm sorry, what?"

Charlie shoots a glare in Hunter's direction. "Aren't you supposed to be at the tree farm?"

Hunter gives him a small smile. "I had to pick a few things up in town and thought I'd drop by for a few minutes."

"It's been a few minutes. You can go."

Charlie tries to shove him out of the booth, but I throw out a hand to stop him.

"Hold on. When did you get drunk in Canada?" Charlie mumbles something to himself that I can't hear. "What was that?"

"He didn't just get drunk in Canada. He got *arrested* in Canada," Hunter supplies.

"You got arrested in Canada? I didn't know that could happen." I laugh.

"Well, it can, and it does. And it's not something I like telling people." Charlie glares at Hunter. *If looks could kill…*

"I don't think I've ever seen you drunk."

"Probably because the one and only time I got drunk, I got arrested," Charlie clarifies.

"But why? Why did you get drunk in Canada of all places?"

"It happened. It was an accident. One that I fully blame on Hunter allowing to happen."

"Hey! It wasn't my fault!" Hunter defends himself.

Charlie nods. "It was, because you kept feeding me shots."

"Again, how did I not know you went to Canada?" I ask.

I know everything about Charlie. I've known him since third grade. How can I not know this fact?

"It was right after you got married and were on your honeymoon."

I wince, not wanting the reminder of anything having to do with my marriage.

"Maybe next time don't take Hunter with you to Canada. This is why you need me in your life. To keep you from doing stupid shit."

"I'd say we should order shots to celebrate," Hunter starts, "but I'd hate for Charlie to get drunk and get arrested here."

"Hunter, as much as I love having you here, it's time to go." Charlie again tries to shove Hunter out of the booth, and this time he succeeds. "See if you drink for free the next time you're here."

"You love me." Hunter blows him a kiss as he waves at me before disappearing out the front door.

"As for you." Charlie pulls me up and I wobble. I've been here for hours, since right after I finished signing the papers, and I've drunk more than I have in a long time. "You're going to go to my house and sleep this off."

I shake my head, the bar spinning. "'S'okay. I'll call a ride share and head to my parents'."

"Brooks."

"Charlie."

I give him the best smile I can muster up today.

"You're being stubborn," he tells me.

"No, I'm not. I'm homeless, jobless, and single. I'm a fucking catch."

"Brooks, you just got divorced. You are not going to be trying to catch another fish anytime soon. Give yourself a break."

"I'll be sure to tell people that next summer when I'm sleeping on a park bench."

"You're staying with me." Charlie waves off my comment. "I won't take no for an answer."

"You realize I come with a seventy-five-pound dog, right?"

"You realize I love Comet, right?" he fires back at me. "Stop arguing with me. Go sleep off your hangover at your parents' and then you can move your stuff in when you're ready."

I wrap Charlie in a warm hug. "This is why you're my best friend."

His breath ghosts my ear as he returns the hug. It's just what I needed right about now. With everything in my life spiraling out of control, it's nice to know I can depend on one person.

My best friend.

My Charlie.

As long as I have him in my life, I'll have everything I need.

Chapter Two

CHARLIE

WHY AM I FRIENDS WITH YOU?

"Hey, Hunter." I stride toward him and drop a peck onto his cheek.

"Charlie." Hunter holds open the door to the Melted Snowman as a wall of heat and the fresh scent of chocolate greet us. "I'd ask how you're doing, but I think I know."

I scoff at him as we head to the counter to order our drinks. "Umm, rude. I'm doing great."

Hunter rolls his eyes as we wait on our peppermint hot chocolates. "Brooks is moving in today, right?"

"Yes."

Hunter gives me a knowing nod, his slouchy, knit hat not doing much to keep his blond hair out of his bright blue eyes. If I didn't know Hunter better, I'd guess he was a surfer from California.

But he hates people and loves the outdoors of Maine.

Grabbing the oversized mug from the barista, I spin on my heel and take in the busy cafe. Red-and-white striped wallpaper is barely visible behind photos of the town that cover the walls. A mishmash of squashy armchairs and tables fill the space. Mini Christmas trees sit on the tables, and garland hangs from the icy windows.

If the Christmas spirit weren't alive and well in me already, I couldn't resist it here.

Spotting a couple leaving, I navigate through the tight space and drop down onto a chair by the window that faces the sidewalk.

"So, you're hiding out with me instead of helping Brooks?" Hunter asks after he sits down across from me. He shrugs out of his jacket, and his denim shirt, with the Naughty Pine Tree Farm logo, is stretched tight across his chest.

"Excuse me!" I jab a finger in his direction. "I am not hiding."

"You're not?" Hunter raises one pointed brow at me.

"Stop it. Brooks didn't want my help."

I take a hearty sip of my cocoa to try and put an end to this conversation. But I'm not that lucky.

"I'm worried about you."

"Why?" I ask. Snow is starting to fall outside the window.

"You know why." Hunter gives me a pointed look.

"It'll be fine."

Hunter snorts over his own sip of his drink. "Fine? Really?"

"I don't know why I'm friends with you. The way you go blabbing things to people that don't need to know it."

"Are you still mad that I told Brooks about you getting drunk in Canada?"

"Excuse me. You told him I got arrested in Canada."

That gets a beaming smile out of Hunter. Or as close to one as he is likely to give. "What? It's funny."

"Not when it's because I was sad Brooks got married."

"And if he gets married again, I'll be sure to take you to Canada and let you get drunk again. And maybe not let you get arrested."

I sigh. "Seriously, why am I friends with you?"

"Because I don't take your bullshit," he tells me. "And I give you a discount on your Christmas tree."

That puts a smile on my face. "I need to come out this week and cut one down."

Hunter shakes his head and leans back in his chair. "You better come quick. All the good trees are going fast."

"You know I can't pick it out too early."

It's always been my tradition since I moved into my house to pick it out after the post-Thanksgiving rush. Too many people going all at once make it hard to study the trees. I want to spend my time with them to pick the very best one. Not necessarily the biggest or the prettiest, but the one that calls to me.

Hunter thinks I'm crazy, but I don't care.

"Well, come soon. Otherwise, you'll get the Charlie Brown tree."

I take a sip of my drink and smack my lips together. Fuck, is this hot cocoa ever delicious. "And I would make it the most beautiful tree in town."

Hunter smiles at me, a small quirk of his lips that's hidden beneath his well-groomed beard. "You would. I dropped off the tree for the tavern on my way over."

"You're the best." I blow a kiss in his direction. "Are you still coming to Ugly Sweater Night?"

Hunter groans. "Are you going to make me? You know how tired I am this time of year."

"Yes. You know I won't take no for an answer."

"Take your new roommate."

"We'll see."

Another eye roll from the tall man across from me.

"Stop judging me. I can feel your judgment from here."

Hunter quirks a brow at me. It's all he has to do. The fucker.

"I'm not judging."

"Yes, you are. I can hear your thoughts from here."

He sips on his peppermint hot chocolate. "Oh yeah? What am I thinking then?"

"That inviting Brooks to live with me is a bad idea because I'm in love with him."

"You said it, not me."

"You suck, you know that?"

The corner of Hunter's mouth quirks up in a half smile. "I haven't been doing much of that lately."

I lean back in the oversized, upholstered chair. "And whose fault is that? How many times have I tried to set you up, Hunter? Hmm?"

"Sue me if I don't want to be set up."

"Maybe if you come to Ugly Sweater Night, you might meet someone."

Hunter groans, scrubbing a hand over his beard. "You are so hard to say no to, you know that, right?"

I give him a playful smile. "It's my superpower."

"Fine. I'll come. But if I'm not having fun after one drink, I'm leaving."

I clap my hands together in excitement. "You'll have a blast. Bring Oliver. He'll have fun."

That brings out a genuine smile when I mention Hunter's best friend in town. "I will pass the message along."

"Good. Now, I need to be getting home. Be a good landlord and greet my houseguest."

Hunter reaches across the table and drops his hand on my arm.

"Look, I'm only saying this because you're my friend, Charlie. You're in love with him. I know he's your best friend, but this is a bad idea. Just because it's Christmas doesn't mean Brooks is going to magically fall in love with you."

"I know that, Hunter," I scoff. "It will be fine."

"Famous last words."

BY THE TIME I leave the Melted Snowman, heavy snow is falling. Bright strands of white lights are wrapped around streetlamps. It looks like live fairies twinkling against the iron posts.

It puts a smile on my face as I shove my hands into my gloves and head through town toward home. Even with the snow, the town is busy. People are moving in and out of the stores. Carolers are standing in the town square serenading tourists and townspeople alike.

This time of year in Moose Falls is always my favorite. No one is unhappy. There's a smile on everyone's face, and there is always something going on. It's one of the best times to visit.

Even though we have a lot of people come and stay during the summer for trips out on the water, it's this time of year that's magical.

I love it.

When my cream and green cedar-shake house comes into view, the smile on my face grows. The sidewalk is already shoveled, and a stream of smoke is coming out from the chimney.

With Brooks moving in today, I took the night off from the Tinsel Tavern. When I offered to help him unpack, he shut me down and told me to get out of the house.

Something about not seeing how little he had left after the divorce.

"Hello?" I call out as I push open the front door. The smell of sugar hits me immediately.

Claws click on the floor as a giant ball of yellow fluff comes running up to me. "Hi, Comet."

I drop down onto my knees to pet him as he throws his paws over my shoulders. His tongue is hanging out of his mouth as I rub his soft fur.

"Someone is happy to see you."

Brooks steps into the small foyer, a kitchen towel thrown over his shoulder. He's dressed in a pair of black sweats and a sweatshirt. With his feet bare, he's made himself at home.

And it has my heart catching in my chest.

"Hey. Did you get settled in?"

Standing, I shrug out of my coat, take off my gloves, and slip out of my boots.

Brooks turns to head into the living room and I follow him. Just like Comet.

It doesn't look like he moved in at all. The living room, with its natural wood walls and high vaulted ceiling, has a few extra books stacked in the built-ins next to the fireplace, but that's it. A new candle is burning on the dining room table, sitting in front of a bay window that overlooks the lake just beyond, and a plate of fresh cookies waiting to be eaten sits on the gray marble counter.

Still like my house, with only a few traces of Brooks's presence.

"I'd say so."

"Wow." I drop into one of the barstools and grab a cookie. Chocolate chip. My favorite. "Did you get everything unpacked?"

Brooks nods, patting Comet before he heads into the second bedroom upstairs. As much as Comet is over here, I've always kept a bed here for him. "A few boxes in my closet, but everything is where it needs to be for now."

I take another bite of the sweet cookie. "You know, you're welcome to stay here as long as you need to."

A sad look washes over his face. "I know, Charlie. But it feels like I can't move on until I get a place of my own, ya know?"

I swallow, the cookie turning bitter. "I know. But the offer still stands."

Brooks winks at me and it does funny things to my insides. "It's why I love you so much, Charlie. Always thinking of others."

I roll my eyes at him to mask the pain that he doesn't mean those words. Well, he loves me as his best friend, but he's not *in* love with me.

"Yeah, yeah."

I stand to go change into something different before cooking dinner, but Brooks stops me with a hand on my arm. "I'm serious, Charlie."

"I know."

Brooks pulls me into a hug, and it has me melting into a puddle. It's quick. A thank you of sorts. I start spiraling. The pine scent of his body wash lingers with his laundry detergent. I can feel the hard muscles of his back under the soft cotton of his hoodie.

Fuck.

I've always been able to keep my feelings for Brooks in

check. Home was my safe space. Sure, Brooks was always over here, but he always went home to his wife.

Now? Now, he'll be here all the time. Twenty-four seven. I don't know if I'm ready for that. If I'm ready for the full-on Brooks assault on all of my senses.

Maybe this was a bad idea.

Chapter Three

BROOKS

TRIFECTA OF SUCKAGE

The kitchen is spotless. Living room? You could eat off the floors. My bedroom? It would pass a drill sergeant's test.

Laundry is done. Hell, I even did Charlie's to try and pass the time.

But glancing at the time on my phone, it's only a little after one in the afternoon. Even after eating lunch, everything is neat and tidy.

If I have no job, I at least want to be the best houseguest I can be for Charlie. Even if it means I'm now doomscrolling on his couch.

I can't help it.

Seeing all the happy posts people are uploading to social media has me spiraling. I shouldn't be on the app, but what else is there to do?

Comet gave up on me sometime after lunch and went

into my room to sleep. When I've lost my dog, I know it's bad.

I don't know how to pull myself out of this mood.

And then I see it.

A photo of Delia and Britney. I forgot Britney had this influencer account. Delia told me that if I followed her, it looked better for her and she'd get more free stuff.

Of course, Delia would go to the Caribbean over the holidays. She always hated that I made her wait until after Christmas.

Sue me for wanting to spend the month leading up to my favorite holiday in my own house. Sun and sand is not how I ever pictured spending my holiday. Snow, hot chocolate, and Christmas trees in my home was always how I spent it.

We always ended up going on my timeline, and maybe that's what led to the downfall of our marriage. I didn't compromise enough. We were two different people who wanted to lead two very different lives.

I loved being in the small town of Moose Falls, but for Delia, it was stifling. No matter what I did to show her how great it could be and the life we could have together, she didn't want it.

Well, I guess she can finally do what she wants.

Fuck. I really need to unfollow her.

"You need to stop."

Charlie reaches over the back of the couch and grabs my phone from my hand.

"Hey!"

Charlie peers at my phone and flashes it back to me. "You're following her best friend's influencer account?"

I can hear the judgment in his tone. Popping up onto my knees, I grab my phone back from him. "I forgot I was. I unfollowed everyone else."

Charlie heads into the kitchen, shaking his head. "It's not healthy for you to sit and stare at social media all day."

"I know that." I flop back onto the couch like a dramatic teenager. "And when did you get home?"

At least he has a job to go to. Having worked for Delia's family's company, even remotely, I also lost my job.

I don't think I've ever been at a lower point in my life.

"I texted to see if you were okay, but you never responded."

Pulling up my texts, I see them.

CHARLIE

Morning! Feeling okay today?

How are you feeling, Brooks? Okay?

Okay, seriously, why aren't you responding?

Did you die? You always text me back immediately.

Okay, if you're dead when I come inside in ten minutes, I'll never forgive you

I WINCE. "SORRY."

"It's okay. I just want to make sure *you're* okay," Charlie calls out from the kitchen.

"It just sucks, ya know?" I tell him. Charlie is the only person I would confess my true feelings to because I feel safe. Every time my parents call, I paste on a happy voice so they don't know how bad I'm really feeling. Being around Charlie is about the one good thing I have going for me right now. "I'm homeless, jobless, and single around my favorite holiday. It's the trifecta of suckage."

Charlie's there, dropping onto his knees and resting his arms on the back of the couch. I stare at my best friend. His brown hair flops into his eyes.

"You're sad."

I snort a laugh. "Stating the obvious, Charlie."

"I'm going to cheer you up."

Sitting up, I rest my chin on the back of the couch. Up close, I can see the determined look in Charlie's eyes. "And how are you going to do that?"

"Easy." Charlie smiles and it reaches his eyes. "We're going to celebrate Christmas together."

"Christmas isn't for another three weeks, Charlie."

"Duh. I'm going to pick out my Christmas tree tomorrow, so you're going to help. Then we'll decorate. We'll make Christmas cookies, sing carols, and watch cheesy Christmas movies. It'll be perfect."

I give him a halfhearted smile. "And after tomorrow?"

"Then we'll go ice skating. Sledding. Paint ornaments. There's plenty we can do to celebrate the holiday," Charlie tells me. There's a determination in his voice.

"You'd really do all of that with me?"

A warmth blooms in my chest. One that feels sneakily like hope. That maybe there's a light at the end of this tunnel.

"Of course I would. You're my best friend."

I give Charlie an awkward pat on the top of his head. "Okay. Let's do it."

"Good." Charlie brushes his hair back into place. "I'm going to make it so you get sick of Christmas."

"Doubt it, but don't let me stop you."

Because for the first time in a long time, I don't feel like I need to be sitting on the couch wasting away my days.

Bring it on, Christmas.

Bring it on.

Chapter Four

CHARLIE

LISTEN TO THE TREES

"I'm surprised you're letting me in on this sacred tradition," Brooks tells me as he hops out of the truck.

"You're about the only person I would. And I still have my concerns."

"Oh yeah? Like what?" Brooks crosses his arms as he leans against the front of the old green pickup truck I use for getting my tree.

I eye him up and down.

The difference between yesterday and today is night and day. Since he moved in, I've barely seen him smile. But today? Today there is one sitting on his face.

Bright and happy. A real smile.

Thank God.

I hate seeing Brooks so down. If I have to let him in on my sacred tradition, so be it.

"If you interrupt me while I'm listening to my trees, I'm sending you home."

Brooks laughs. "Okay. No talking while you're listening to the trees."

"And no rolling your eyes at me if it's taking too long or asking when we're leaving."

"Check and check." Brooks makes two check marks in the air. "I'll follow you around like a little puppy and tell Hunter when we're ready."

"Ready for what?" a familiar voice calls out.

The man in question greets us at the main gate. A small wooden shack serves as the entrance to rows and rows of trees as far as the eye can see. A welcome sign, painted like a candy cane and lit up with Christmas lights, greets visitors. A little ways down the path is a small train to take kids and their parents on rides throughout the farm.

The Naughty Pine Tree Farm in all her glory.

Hunter's pride and joy. People from all over south-western Maine come to get their Christmas trees from Hunter. I don't know how he grows them, but they are a cut above the rest.

"Ready to cut down our tree," I tell Hunter.

"You brought Brooks with you?" He raises a brow at me.

"Yes." I grab Brooks by the arm. "Now, if you'll excuse us, we're going Christmas tree hunting."

"Have fun!" Hunter calls out behind us.

After stopping at the small booth to get us hot choco-lates, I trudge through the snow with Brooks nipping at my heels.

"Why are we not looking at these trees?" Brooks asks.

"Because there are too many people here."

I dodge a family with little kids that are eyeing a

healthy looking spruce. Something I've come to learn over the years of picking out my own trees.

There are so many more varieties than just pine.

"Okay, so where are we going then?" Brooks asks.

"To my spot."

Brooks doesn't say anything but just sips his hot chocolate as I lead us farther and farther away from the crowds. The small lights that hang from wooden poles cast each tree in an ethereal glow.

Now that it's quieter back here, it's easier to be among the trees. Without as many people, I can examine each tree. See where there are holes. What ones might look sick.

Not that Hunter has bad trees, but sometimes there are ones that aren't up to par.

"What about this one?" Brooks asks.

He's standing next to a large fir, full at the base and tapering off to the perfect top. I can see my rainbow angel sitting on top of that tree.

"It doesn't speak to me."

"Okay." I can see him fight a smile. One that says he wants to comment further, but he doesn't.

I run my gloved hands through the needles on each tree as we walk up and down the rows.

When I stop suddenly, Brooks bumps into me.

"Did you find one?" he whispers into my ear.

I ignore how the sudden warmth makes me feel because the tree at the end of the row is just what I'm looking for.

It's tall, well past nine feet. It'll look perfect in my living room with the vaulted ceilings. It's full at the bottom and the needles are just right to the touch.

Pick me this tree is telling me. It has a smile bursting on my face.

"This is the one."

"It's perfect," Brooks confirms.

I spin around, and Brooks is impossibly close to me. I need some cool air to separate the two of us, so I take a step back. "Make sure no one takes it. I'll go find Hunter."

Brooks winks at me, and it does funny things to my insides. "I'll guard our tree with my life."

Our tree.

Fuck. I hate this. I really do.

It's easy to see how this could be our life together. Picking out Christmas trees together. Cozying up in front of the fire with Comet. Getting wrapped up in bed together.

But it's not.

This is not real life. It's only a fantasy until Brooks can get his own place and find some stability in his life.

I need to pop this bubble before I get too swept up in it.

"Hey." Hunter is shaking hands with a family as they set off with their tree. "Can you help us?"

Hunter crosses his arms as he approaches me. "I don't know. Can I?"

"What's that supposed to mean?"

"You know what it means. I think this is a bad idea, Charlie."

"And I told you, I don't care."

Hunter walks away from me, carrying a saw. "Don't come crying to me when it all goes south."

"You're such a grinch!" I tell him, following him to the cart that will take us to where I left Brooks.

"Just trying to keep your feet on the ground."

I hop up and sit next to him. "My feet are just fine, thank you."

The wind blows around us as Hunter steers us in the direction I came from. I'm thankful for the distraction and him not pestering me about Brooks.

"You would find the best tree in the entire lot," Hunter confirms when he sees where Brooks is standing as we pull up to him.

"You know, I don't know if I've ever been back this far," Brooks tells us as Hunter starts to saw down the base. This far out, the trees aren't precut.

"We have a lot of space here, with more than just the tree lots."

"Really?" Brooks asks. "I guess I figured you're only busy at Christmas time."

Hunter steps back, wiping his brow. "That's partially my fault. I don't do a good job advertising. We get by, but I could do more."

A light shines in Brooks's eyes. "You know, I went to school for marketing."

"Really?" Hunter asks. His eyes flit to mine to confirm, and I give him a nod.

Brooks nods. "I did. If you want some help, I could take a look at your website and offer some advice."

"Hunter doesn't have a website," I offer. "Only social media."

Hunter cuts me a glare.

"Not one that is public. I don't understand how to build them and could use the help. I want to expand and do more in the offseason to bring people here and—"

"Let me help. I'm really good at it. It'd give me something to do, even if it's only temporary," Brooks says, eagerness hanging on every word.

"Just like that?" Hunter laughs.

"If it means I'm not sitting on Charlie's couch every day, I'm game."

"Great." Hunter sticks his hand out for Brooks to shake.

"Aww. Look at that. My two favorite people working together."

"Don't make it weird, Charlie. It's a job," Hunter tells me.

"But you're helping out Brooks in his time of need. I knew there was a good person under there." I pat the jacket over Hunter's heart.

Hunter swats me away. "Fuck you. I'm a very nice person."

"Just kidding." I blow a kiss in his direction. "I know you are."

Brooks goes back around to the tree, grabbing the saw and helping out with cutting it down.

"Thank you, Hunter. I know this means a lot to Brooks," I whisper.

"And to you."

"And to me. I appreciate you helping him out."

Hunter nudges my side. "Look, I might not be on board with your whole plan, but I can certainly help Brooks out."

"Thank you."

A light snow starts falling as we load the tree into the cart to take back to the main gate. I watch as Hunter and Brooks chat for a few minutes.

With the Christmas lights sparkling, it's a magical night.

This is why I love the Naughty Pine Tree Farm and the holiday season.

Because even if you're going through a hard time, things can still be magical. If only you open your eyes and look for it.

Chapter Five

CHARLIE

THE BEST LOOKING THING ON MY TREE

"How did I not know you have *this* many Christmas decorations?" Brooks whines as he sets yet another box down on the living room floor. "I mean, I love Christmas, but you?"

"Stop it." I swat at him. "You've never been with me to decorate."

Brooks laughs. "Probably because I would've been buried under decorations and then hung up on the tree like an ornament."

I give my best friend a syrupy sweet smile. "You'd be the prettiest ornament on my tree."

Brooks winks at me before heading up to his room to grab his own décor. Untangling a box of garlands, I watch as Brooks bounds down the stairs.

"That's all you have?" I'm flabbergasted at the one

small, clear tote he brings out. "What happened to everything else?"

Brooks shrugs a shoulder. "It's all I wanted to keep after the divorce. Everything else we bought together, but this was mine and I couldn't get rid of it."

My heart clangs around in my chest for my best friend. Fucking Delia. I hate her. I mean, I've always had it out for her because she got Brooks and I didn't, but seeing the number she did on him?

I hate her.

"We'll make sure it's front and center then." I bump my shoulder against his.

"You're the best friend I could have ever asked for."

Brooks's words warm me from the inside out as he peels the lid off the container. It's a mishmash of ornaments, knickknacks, and a special collar for Comet, complete with a bow tie.

"And don't you forget it."

"How could I?" Brooks's face lights up. "If you need proof of that, check this out."

Brooks holds something up for me to see.

"I didn't know you still had this."

I grab the frame from his hand, looking at the picture of us from high school. It was maybe our junior year, and the two of us thought it would be a good idea to make our own ugly sweaters to wear to school. With the other's face on our own sweater.

It's the faces of two skinny kids, each wearing their best friend's face proudly on their chest. It was one of my favorite Christmases because I loved that I could be so ridiculous with Brooks and he would never judge me for it.

"It's one of my favorites," Brooks tells me, looking at the photo with me. It made me fall that much harder for him back then, and with his clean scent mixing with the fresh pine, my heart speeds up.

I sigh, setting the picture down on the bookshelf.

"Maybe we should make some more ugly sweaters for this year and wear them on Christmas morning."

Brooks bursts out laughing. "Yes. We have to. Maybe we can even make one for Comet to wear."

Comet lifts his head up to see what we're doing before going back to his bone that I picked up for him.

"Deal."

The two of us work together, hanging tinsel on the tree that glimmers in the colored lights we hung earlier this morning.

"For someone that loves his tree so much, I'm surprised your ornaments aren't perfectly matched," Brooks tells me, hanging an ornament that I hand painted a few years ago.

A merman with a rainbow fin.

"Because,"—I straighten the ornament—"all of them hold special meaning."

"What meaning does a half-naked mermaid have?" Brooks laughs.

"Mer*man*," I correct, poking him in his muscular abs. "You just wish your abs were as good-looking as this."

Brooks pulls his hoodie up, flashing me his stomach.

Fuck. Me. I should not have started this. How does Brooks not know the way he has me drooling over him?

"I think they are."

"These?" I feel around on his stomach against my better judgment as Brooks shies away from me. "I'd need a map to find them."

"I guess you just have a thing for mermen."

"Don't make fun of him." I push Brooks out of the way with a hip check. "This was a fundraiser night we did at the tavern. Donate five dollars and you get to paint your own ornament. It was a huge success and it helped people in need over the holidays."

Brooks studies me. "You're a good person, in case no one has told you that."

His words make me blush. "Thanks."

"And because you're a good person, please tell me you are going to do that again."

"Maybe."

"Pleeeease?" Brooks pleads. "I want to do it. I want to paint a merman and put ridiculous tattoos all over his chest."

Brooks pokes at the one now hanging on the tree.

"If I say yes, will that mean you won't paint the merman I already have?"

He nods. "Yes."

"Then I'll make it happen."

"Best. Friend. Ever."

A furious blush is now creeping up my cheeks even farther.

Get it together, Charlie, I chide myself.

I watch as Brooks hangs ornaments all over the tree. There is no rhyme or reason to it, and it's why I love my tree so much.

It's not perfect. Far from it, actually.

But it's perfect to me. The memories that cling to the pine branches are of all the holidays, trips, and events that mean more to me than anything else.

By the time we're done, it's early evening and the sun has already set. The house smells of sugar from the cookies we made plus the scent of the fresh tree now taking up one corner of the living room. It's like an explosion of Christmas and I love it.

Garlands hang from the fireplace with Brooks's stocking holders sitting on the mantel. Christmas throw pillows now cover the couch. Knickknacks line the book-shelves. Every single space in the house has something Christmas on it.

With the snow falling outside and Comet happily chewing on a candy cane-shaped bone in front of the fire, it's the epitome of a magazine spread inside my house.

After making two cups of hot chocolate with a dash of peppermint schnapps, I carry them into the living room and hand one to Brooks.

Before he even takes a sip, he grabs both cups and sets them down onto the coffee table and pulls me into a hug. I don't know if I'll ever get over just how good he smells.

"Thank you for this, Charlie."

"You never have to thank me. I'm always here for you."

I squeeze Brooks a little tighter, savoring this moment. I know Brooks will eventually move on.

It doesn't mean I can't make the most of the time we have together. I'll give Brooks the perfect holiday he deserves if it's the last thing I do.

Then move on.

Even if I might break my own heart in the process.

Chapter Six

BROOKS

UGLY SWEATER FEELINGS

The sound of the front door opening has me leaning back from the counter. Paws echo on the hardwood floor as Charlie's voice coos down at Comet.

"Hey," I call out. "You're home earlier than I expected."

"Everyone had things under control at the bar, so I wasn't needed." He shrugs out of his black puffer coat and hangs it on the hook next to the front door before walking into the kitchen.

Snow sticks to Charlie's hair and pink blossoms on his cheeks. His brown eyes are happy.

Why am I noticing these things about him?

Ever since we decorated the tree, it seems a switch has been flipped. When he touched my abs, it's like a zap of electricity flooded my veins.

Charlie was playing around. I know that. But it addled my brain more than I care to admit.

Maybe it's because I'm in a weird limbo right now. Living with my best friend while I try to get back on my feet. Trying to recover from the divorce.

That has to be it. At least, that's what I keep telling myself.

"What's for dinner?" Charlie asks, sidling up next to me.

"Rice bowls. I figure I can make cookies later before we make our sweaters."

Charlie groans. "I love you, Brooks, but I cannot eat another cookie."

"Hey!" I'm indignant. "What do you have against my cookies?"

"Nothing." He smirks, rubbing his stomach. "But I cannot keep eating cookies every night."

I wave him off, ignoring the way my eyes dart down to his stomach. *Again, why am I noticing these things?* "It's the holidays. You should get to eat all the cookies you want."

"I feel like that's not something you'd hear a parent say."

"Speaking of. My mom called today and asked when your parents would be in town for the holidays. They want to get together for dinner with us."

Charlie grabs a sparkling water from the fridge and opens his drink, taking a long gulp. "They're coming in the week before Christmas, I think. Maybe we can do something around then."

I nod. "Sounds good. I'll let her know. They still have no desire to come back to Maine?"

"No. My mom is done with the cold weather and wants the beach."

I spoon two cups of rice into the bowls and start piling

toppings onto each. "I don't know if you could ever get me to leave Moose Falls."

"There's nowhere else you'd want to live?"

"Been there, done that." Having gone to college in New York, I realized that the only place I want to live is Moose Falls. "I'm a lifer. Just like you."

"Worse places to be stuck," Charlie tells me, accepting his dinner from me. "Not that I think I'm stuck."

"Cheers to that." I grab my water and clink my glass with his.

"How's work going with Hunter?"

"Good." I take a bite of dinner and chew. "Really good, actually."

"Yeah?" Charlie asks.

I nod. "He needs more help than I thought, so it's nice to feel needed."

Charlie gives me a warm smile. I don't need to ask what it's about. For the first time since I moved in with Charlie and the divorce was finalized, I feel like things are looking up.

"If you can even get him a functioning website, it will be better than anything else he currently has. I know he wants to expand."

I nod, taking another bite. "We've talked about ways he can expand using it as a platform. I'm excited about his ideas."

"I'm glad you can help him."

After eating the rest of our meals in a companionable silence, I grab our bowls—now empty—and drop them into the sink.

"Are you ready?"

Charlie rubs his hands together with a gleeful smile on his face. "I am. Are you?"

"You bet."

Charlie hops off the stool at the island and walks over to the dining room table where tonight's activity is all laid out.

"I can't believe you found a dog sweater we can decorate for Comet," I tell Charlie, holding up the soft, green material.

Charlie laughs. "Finding the right size was the hardest part."

"It just means we can make it even more ridiculous."

When I suggested this, I didn't think he'd take it up with such zeal. But that's my Charlie. He doesn't do anything half-assed.

Puff balls and garlands and glitter glue sit on the table. He even has small jingle bells for us to choose from.

"Are you trying to put a bell on me?" I grab one of the small objects and listen to its melodic sound.

"Yes, so I always know where you are." Charlie grabs it from my hand. "Maybe we should put some of these on Comet's sweater."

"Let's work on his and then we can work on ours."

"Yours is the green one to match Comet."

"Aww. Like father, like son."

Charlie shakes his head at me as we make quick work of decorating Comet's before moving onto each of our own.

"What are you doing on yours?" I ask Charlie, peeking over his shoulder.

"No looking." Charlie shifts so I can't see what he's putting on his sweater.

"It's not a test. I'm not going to cheat."

"I don't want you copying my greatness."

"If that's what we're calling these sweaters." I laugh.

"You know…" Charlie reaches across me for the green puff glitter. "We'll have to wear these on Friday."

"What's on Friday?" I ask.

"We're having an Ugly Sweater Party."

I laugh, dabbing glue onto another puff ball and putting it next to a fake Christmas light. "Will there be a contest for best sweater?"

"Yes."

"Then count me in."

"I hate to say, but you'll probably win."

"Hey!" I smack him in the arm. "This is a thing of beauty."

"Umm…okay."

I stare at the back of his head. "It's not like you can see it."

Charlie spins on his heel to take mine in. "Oh, Brooks."

I peer over his shoulder and look at his. Of course it's a masterpiece. All the garland is done up in a pattern with balls placed over the sweater to look like a tree.

"How can yours look so good?" I balk. "Seriously. It looks like something you'd buy at the store."

Charlie reaches across the table and grabs one of the star patches. He dabs some glue on it before adding it right below the collar. "Because I'm amazing."

"Show-off," I mutter.

Charlie laughs before calling Comet over. "No one is going to look cuter than Comet."

Charlie undoes the Velcro straps to put Comet's sweater on over his back. He even bought a little Santa hat for him to wear.

His tongue is hanging out of his mouth as he sits in his sweater like we didn't just put the most ridiculous thing on him.

"You're right," I confirm. "No one is going to look cuter than he does."

"Which means he needs to stay at home for the party."

"Not like you can allow dogs in the tavern anyway." I laugh. "But we need a picture to show the guys how cute he is."

I don't waste another second and slide my green sweater on over my head. The minute Charlie looks at me, he bursts out laughing.

"Oh my God, Brooks. It's even worse on you."

"You mean it looks even better and I make Christmas sweaters sexy."

Charlie tries not to laugh. "Whatever you say."

Tiny, glittery puff balls in all sizes dot my sweater. A garland rests in ropes on the front with random patches pasted all over.

Charlie takes more care in putting his on as we both squat next to Comet. Pulling my phone out of my pocket, I switch to selfie mode.

"Say 'Brooks has the best Christmas sweater ever!'"

"Brooks has the ugliest sweater ever!" Charlie claps back as Comet lets out a bark when I take the picture.

Looking at the screen, it's the two of us in a nutshell. A smile lights up my face as Charlie is caught mid-word, with Comet's chin taking up most of the picture.

I'll never delete this one, but I take a second one where we're all looking.

"Better?" I hold my phone out to Charlie.

He studies the photo, a look washing over his face that I can't quite read. Which is weird, because I can always read him. What's he thinking right now?

Is he happy? Sad? Over this ridiculous thing?

It's confusing that I can't read him right now. Made even more confusing by these feelings I'm having. It's like one of these tiny, glittery balls has dislodged itself and planted itself in my brain, the fuzzy parts making my own head feel the same way.

Clearing his throat, he looks at me before putting some space between us. "Comet looks great."

"He does."

A ball drops off my sweater.

Charlie grabs it and tries to press it back on. "Well, maybe we shouldn't have put these on immediately."

"Lesson learned. Next time we make ugly sweaters, we let them dry."

"We'll still beat the guys."

"Bring it on, Charlie. Bring it on."

Chapter Seven

TRUTH OR DARE

"You really are no fun," I tell Theo as he helps me with drinks.

I don't miss the way he gives my sweater a slow once-over. "And you went overboard on your sweater."

"Please. You're just jealous you don't have a sweater as amazing as mine."

In fact, he doesn't have a sweater at all. He's wearing a denim shirt tucked into a pair of ripped black pants. He looks good, even if he ignored the dress code for the evening.

"Maybe I should agree with you since you're giving us free drinks," Theo tells me.

"Please. You know you love hanging at the tavern. Ugly sweaters and all."

It's one of the many reasons I opened this place. I

wanted a place where my friends and I could hang out without being judged. A safe space.

It's become one of the more popular bars in Moose Falls. People of all orientations come to hang out.

But the thing I love most? I can be here with my friends and socialize while keeping an eye on things even on my night off.

What can I say? I love my job and The Tinsel Tavern.

"Is this a new drink?" Theo asks, grabbing one of the glasses from the tray I just set down. The pinkish-orange liquid glimmers in the disco ball lights as the music changes to a fast-paced Christmas tune.

"The Naughty but Nice. I made it with whiskey tonight instead of vodka."

The Naughty but Nice is one of my favorite cocktails we serve. With orange juice, cranberry, and ginger, it cuts the whiskey to give it a sweeter taste. Add in a splash of club soda and it's perfect.

"Cheers, everyone."

We all clink our glasses together at the large, round table where we are gathered instead of our usual booth in the back of the bar.

Glancing around at all of my friends, I'm glad we're all together. The smile on Brooks's face right now makes it worth it.

He's had a rough few weeks, so this makes me happy.

Theo and Griffin are arguing about something while Hunter and Oliver are whispering to each other.

Brooks is sitting next to me, watching all of this with a smile on his face. Him coming out with me and my friends was always a rare occasion. He always said Delia wanted him home.

I'm happy I get this time with him now.

"Why are you staring at me like that?" Brooks asks, interrupting my train of thought.

"It's nice seeing you happy is all."

"I have you to thank for that."

I blush at his words, sipping on my drink. "I don't like it when you're sad."

Brooks shakes his head. "Hopefully all of that is behind me."

"Alright, I think we should play truth or dare," Griffin pipes up, drumming his hands on the table to grab everyone's attention.

Theo laughs at his friend. "You're so immature."

"What?" Griffin throws his hands up. "It's fun and I'm feeling frisky tonight."

Theo looks at all of us. "I'm sorry. If I knew this was how he was going to be tonight, I would have left him at home."

Griffin gives him a playful shove. "Hey! I resent that."

Hunter snorts. "I'd be game."

That has me nearly spurting out my drink. "You? Really?"

"Really? Truth or dare?" Brooks grumbles.

Hunter passes him another shot. "What, can't handle it?"

Brooks snorts a laugh before knocking back the shot of tequila in one long gulp. I do my best to ignore the way his throat works as he swallows it down.

"I can. I haven't played it since high school."

Hunter leans back in his chair and drapes an arm around Oliver's shoulder. Oliver, in his thick glasses, stares back at his best friend with a soft smile.

Huh. I wonder when that started.

"Good." Hunter eggs him on. "I'd hate for you to chicken out on me."

Brooks reaches across the table to grab another shot and sucks it down.

"No chickening out here."

"Okay, enough, you two," I interrupt them. "Oliver, truth or dare."

"Me? Why are you starting with me?"

Hunter drops his chair back down to the floor and leans across the table. "I'm going first."

I roll my eyes at him. It's just like Hunter to step in for his best friend. Games like this have always made Oliver nervous for as long as I've known him. "Of course you are. Truth or dare?"

"Truth."

"When was your last one-night stand?"

"Charlie! You can't ask that," Oliver chides him.

Hunter pats Oliver's hand that rests on the table. "It's okay. I can answer." Hunter gives me a pointed glare. "If you must know, it was this past fall."

"What?" Oliver gapes at him. "Why didn't you tell me about this?"

Hunter shrugs. "I mean, it was a one-night stand. Picked up a guy here and we had sex. Not much to talk about."

"You're so casual about sex," Oliver tells him.

As one of the servers walks by, Hunter orders multiple shots for everyone. "Ollie. It doesn't have to be a big thing. It can be about two people getting off and moving on."

"But…" His mouth hangs open in shock. Ollie's hazel eyes are wide. Even in the dim light of the bar, I can see how bright red his ears are turning from here. Poor guy. He's just had his mind blown.

"You just need to get laid, Ollie." Griffin reaches across the table and pushes his mouth closed.

"Leave him alone, Griff," Hunter chides him.

"I don't…I don't need to get laid," Ollie sputters.

"Take a shot." Brooks pushes one toward him. "It'll help you feel better."

Ollie grabs one and proceeds to down it immediately, coughing around it. He's never been one to drink while we're out, always opting for water, but tonight, apparently, he needs it.

"Okay, Hunter, you're up. Ask someone."

I get the focus back to the game so Ollie doesn't feel so awkward. Not that I know how he's feeling, but I don't want him to have all the attention on him. He's never been comfortable with it.

"Brooks. Truth or dare."

"Truth."

There's a gleam in Hunter's eyes as he flits his gaze from me to Brooks. The way the corner of his mouth ticks up into a small smile tells me I am not going to like what he asks.

Which makes me nervous.

Hunter leans across the table, glass in hand as he takes a sip before setting his drink down and pointing at Brooks.

"Have you ever been interested in a man before?"

"Hunter!" I admonish him. "Really?"

"What?" He shrugs. "It's an innocent enough question."

"Down, Charlie," Brooks tells me, resting a hand on my forearm that sits on the table. "I'm a big boy. I can answer."

"Then give us your answer," Hunter prods him.

"Yes."

"You have to answer," I tell Brooks, sipping on my own drink.

Brooks looks at me like I've lost my mind. "That was my answer."

I choke over my drink, coughing and trying not to spit it out over everyone sitting at the table. "I'm sorry, what?"

The music of the bar echoes in my ears. The flashing lights blur together and the alcohol in my stomach sours.

Brooks was interested in a man?

I'm going to be sick.

"I think this needs details," Griffin tells us. "I'm kind of surprised by this. Because had I known you liked men, I might've tried something."

"Wait, what?" This time, my head spins to Griffin. He was interested in Brooks? What is going on tonight? Have I entered an alternate universe?

"What?" Griffin shrugs. "Brooks is hot. I think we can all admit that."

The man in question blushes and ignores him. "It was my freshman year roommate."

Andrew? Aaron? I don't even remember his name.

"We got drunk one night and ended up making out," Brooks starts. "I don't know if it was a college thing, but we fooled around a few times. I didn't really get to explore that side of me because right before I came home for Thanksgiving, I met Delia."

I remember that holiday well. All Brooks could talk about was Delia.

Delia this. Delia that. Delia, Delia, Delia.

Fucking *Delia*.

I hated it. It was the first time he was ever serious about anyone. I remember putting on a happy face when he talked about it, but I cried when we both went back to school.

Reaching across the table, I grab my own shot. And then another.

Brooks fooled around with a guy in college?

"Anyone need more shots? I'll go get us some more."

I push away from the table, ignoring the nearly full tray sitting right in front of me.

I need air.

I ignore all the people waving at me as I stumble through the bar and out the back door. A heavy snow is falling from the sky. The cold air burns my lungs, but it's exactly what I need right now.

Tears sting my eyes.

To say my world has been completely rocked tonight isn't an understatement.

Brooks and Asher? Because of course now I remember his name.

Asher with his perfectly coifed hair and solid muscles. That polo he always wore with the popped collar and perfectly pressed jeans.

Of course that is the kind of guy Brooks would be into.

Not scrawny ol' me with my skinny jeans and old band T-shirts. Well, now my mostly plaid shirts and Tinsel Tavern black tee.

"You okay?" Hunter asks, disrupting my spiraling thoughts.

"What the hell were you playing at in there? Hmm?" I spin on my heel, turning my anger toward Hunter. "What was the point of that? Were you trying to make me feel like shit?"

Hunter throws up his hands in defense. "I didn't actually think it would—"

"Would what?" I cut him off. "Prove once and for all that Brooks isn't into men, or that he's just not into *me*?"

"Charlie."

Could this night get any worse?

"Just leave me alone."

Hunter at least has the gall to look chagrined. "I'm sorry, Charlie. I didn't know this would happen."

"That you'd break my heart because after all this time it turns out being in love with my best friend is never going to amount to anything because he just wasn't into *me*?"

"Uhh, guys?"

That voice.

Oh, fuck me.

Brooks.

I guess this night could get worse.

Chapter Eight

TOO MUCH TRUTH

"I'll go check on him." Hunter groans as he stands and follows the path Charlie just cut through the bar. My eyes lock on to his retreating form.

"What do you think that was all about?" I ask the guys as Hunter stalks off after Charlie. I don't know what caused Charlie to bolt from the table so fast.

"Is that the first time you've ever told anyone about your roommate?" Oliver asks, pushing his glasses farther up the bridge of his nose.

"Yeah, but I'm not ashamed of it, if that's what you're getting at." Every single one of these guys is gay or bi. Growing up, it was a normal thing here, so I never thought twice about it.

But I didn't really have time to explore that side of me.

The last I heard, Asher was living in South Carolina with his wife and two kids. Maybe it was him experimenting in college. I always chalked it up to that since I met Delia so soon after.

Everything with Delia was new and fun. I fell hard and fast for her. I couldn't think about anything but her. Maybe that's why we burned out the way we did.

At the beginning, it was all about her. Once we settled into life together, it got stagnant and stale. We fell into our own routines and didn't appreciate one another like we should have.

"Is that the first time you told *Charlie* about that?" Theo asks.

"I mean, I thought he knew."

Right?

Fuck. Maybe I never did tell him because of Delia.

"Damn it. I need to find him."

"And if you want to fool around, you have my number." Griffin winks at me.

"Thanks for the offer, but I'm not looking."

Griffin gives me a slow perusal. "That's a damn shame. I wouldn't mind a one-night stand with you."

"Griffin!" Oliver chides him. "You can't say those things. That's rude."

"Nah," I brush his comments off. "I've heard worse out of him."

"See? I'm a peach."

Oliver shakes his head at him as I stand and weave my way through the crowded bar. I saw both Charlie and Hunter flee through one of the back exit doors.

The door is cracked open, and I hear the tail end of their conversation.

"I'm sorry, Charlie. I didn't know this would happen," I hear Hunter say.

"That you'd break my heart because after all this time it turns out being in love with my best friend is never going to amount to anything because he just wasn't into *me*?"

Oh, shit. I shouldn't be hearing this, but I can't stand here and continue to listen to this conversation between them. Pulling open the door, I interrupt the conversation.

"Uhh, guys?"

Charlie's eyes snap to mine and go wide as saucers. "Brooks."

"I'm just going to go back inside." Hunter slides past me as the door clicks shut behind him.

"Are you okay?"

My head is spinning at what I just overheard.

"I'm fine."

Charlie tries to brush past me to go inside, but I grab his arm, stopping him in his tracks. Tears, or maybe the cold, sting his eyes. Snow clings to his hair.

"No, you're not."

"Just let it go, Brooks."

"We have to talk about this."

Charlie shakes me off. "No, we don't."

"Charlie—"

He's inside before I can argue with him.

Charlie's been in love with me? Since when?

I scrub a hand down my face and watch the snow fall in the street lamps. My mind is spinning. How in the world did I not know this?

Memories of Charlie throughout the years flash through my mind. I moved to Moose Falls in third grade and ever since, Charlie has been in my life.

Walking to school together. Playing soccer together as kids. Telling him things I never told anyone.

I never once got the impression that he loved me, but was I just oblivious?

At least, until last week when I started feeling new

things for him. Why in the hell is all of this coming to the surface now of all times?

A wind blows through, sending a biting cold through me.

Life has been nothing but change lately. Huge, gut-punching life changes.

Through it all, Charlie has been one of the few constants. He held my hand—figuratively—during the entire process. He was there for me.

Now discovering this?

I don't go back inside for my coat. I know the short walk to Charlie's from here will only take a couple of minutes. Right now, I can't be around other people.

Because, for the second time in a month, my world has tilted on its axis.

Because of Charlie.

Snow crunches under my shoes as I walk the familiar path toward Charlie's house.

I wasn't supposed to hear that confession. It wasn't meant for me. But I heard it. I don't know how I can ever *unhear* it.

Fuck.

Large flakes soak through my sweater as the house comes into view. The living room light glows softly.

Comet is at the door as I step inside. "Hey, buddy."

I let him run out to do his business and play in the snow. Watching him settles me. At least, as much as possible right now.

Fuck.

What the hell am I going to do?

I don't know, but everything has changed.

I only hope Charlie and I can figure this out.

Because I'm not ready to lose him.

Chapter Nine

IN FOR A PENNY...

Charlie's avoiding me.

For the better part of the last week, he's been absent. It feels like I saw him more during college with us going to different schools than I've seen him while living with him.

The only reason I know he's been home is my coat appeared on the hook sometime after he came home from the bar that night.

Since I started working at the Naughty Pine, I'm up early while Charlie is still asleep. By the time I get home, he's already at the Tinsel Tavern.

I was hoping we could have a conversation like adults about what I overheard. But if I want to have this conversation, I guess I'm going to have to track him down and force him to have it.

I've gone over this in my head a million different ways

since he walked away from me. The pain in his eyes has haunted me.

Fuck. It has me rubbing the heel of my hand over my heart. The very last thing in the world that I want to do is hurt Charlie.

He's the best person I know. My favorite person in the world.

I can't lose him. And I don't want to let this fester any longer. Hearing his confession is only adding to my own confused feelings.

Maybe if he would talk to me, I'd know what he's feeling. Then I could tell him what's going on inside of me. Because these last few weeks have been nothing short of confusing.

I make a decision. Fuck it.

"I'll be back later, okay, Comet?"

My dog barely opens an eye from his bed in front of the Christmas tree before closing it and going back to snoring.

Grabbing my coat and keys, I stuff my feet into my boots and head toward the Tinsel Tavern.

No more ignoring me. No more avoiding.

It's not like he's the only one that's scared. Charlie's my best friend. If he's nervous or scared about how I'm feeling, we need to talk about that. It's not like he's the only one experiencing these emotions. I'm scared too.

It's a warmer night for Moose Falls with groups of tourists and townspeople alike milling around, drinking hot chocolate and listening to carolers on the street.

I bypass all of them and set my eyes on where I know I'll find my best friend.

The courtyard to the left of the building is filled with people and heaters. Christmas lights woven through the rafters outside cast a soft glow out onto the street.

I nod to the security guy who sits inside the door as I let my eyes adjust to the flashing lights inside.

There. Behind the bar, slinging drinks.

Charlie has a bright smile on his face as he sets a cocktail down in front of someone. The dance floor is packed to the brim with people as a Christmas tune plays out.

My eyes stay fixed on Charlie as I cut through the mass of people. Now that I'm here, my nerves are starting to jumble because I have no idea how this conversation is going to go.

I know the minute he sees me because the smile slides off his face.

Fuck. Okay, this isn't going to go well based on that reaction.

I'm not going to let him run anymore.

"What are you doing here?" Charlie asks, almost yelling over the music.

"You're avoiding me."

"I'm working," he corrects me. "You want something to drink?"

"Beer."

Charlie nods. He knows exactly what I like. It has warmth blooming in my chest. Charlie knows everything about me. It's why he's been my best friend my entire life.

I watch as he grabs a pint glass and pulls the light amber liquid. I'm noticing things about him now that I've never noticed before. The way his biceps move when he draws the tap toward him. The happy smile on his face when a regular calls out to him.

It's everything that makes him my Charlie.

When he sets it in front of me, he is fast to walk away.

"Charlie, can we please talk?" I call after him.

"Busy." He shakes his head, not turning around.

Okay then.

This is going to be harder than I thought.

I have all night though. I'm not going anywhere. If Charlie thinks I'm going to leave, he doesn't know how stubborn I can be.

I'll close this bar down if I have to.

I watch as Charlie mixes and pours drinks. He works effortlessly with his crew behind the bar. It's mesmerizing to watch.

"Can I get you anything?" someone pops up in front of me and asks.

Looking down, my glass is empty. "Sure. Another IPA."

"You got it."

When I go back to searching out Charlie, I see him with someone at the end of the bar. That perks my attention up.

I don't miss the way the guy leans in closer to Charlie. His finger swirls along the rim of his glass as his eyes roam over Charlie's face in what looks like a soft caress.

Whatever the guy says has Charlie throwing his head back in laughter before resting his hand on his forearm. Even from here, I can see how Charlie's fingers brush over his skin. It pulls the guy's attention to that spot.

I have no idea who the man he's talking with is. Well, flirting. Based on how Charlie is reacting, they are definitely flirting.

What. The. Fuck.

A growl bursts out of my chest. I can't get Charlie to talk to me for two minutes—his best friend that he's known his entire life—and he's paying attention to this fool?

And why do I want to be that guy?

Fuck that.

But before I can go interrupt them like a jealous boyfriend, Charlie is rounding the bar and linking hands with this guy and heading to the dance floor.

Again. What the fuck?

Shouldn't he be working?

Perks of being the owner. I can hear Charlie's words echoing in my head.

Fuck. I eye the man he's dancing with. He's attractive, there's no doubt about that. Exactly Charlie's type.

Dark hair. Dark eyes.

The exact opposite of me.

My eyes don't leave them as the music changes to something sexier.

I sip my beer as I watch the guy rest his hands on Charlie's hips.

Fuck. The two of them are moving to the music together, rocking their hips into one another. Charlie's hands slip into the guy's back pockets as they keep dancing.

A burning fire erupts in my gut.

I swallow down the rest of my beer to cool myself off because I have no idea why I'm feeling this way watching Charlie dance with some stranger.

Seriously. What the fuck is wrong with me?

The guy spins Charlie, so now he's facing my direction. The flashing lights are dancing across his face, highlighting all his best features.

The guy splays his hands on Charlie's abs over his T-shirt.

Seriously?

I came here to talk to Charlie and he's ignoring me. Maybe this wasn't a good idea. Because all it's doing is making my gut churn.

It's then I notice the guy's hand is dipping just below Charlie's belt.

Am I jealous? Do I want to be the one dancing with Charlie?

No. It's because the guy is taking advantage of him.

I'm ready to head out there and punch the guy. Let him know he can't do this to my best friend. It's like my thoughts are a beacon to Charlie as his gaze meets mine.

His brown eyes are filled with lust, and it sends a new feeling floating through me. One that I've only ever felt for one other guy.

But now I'm feeling those things for Charlie.

My best friend.

Desire. Lust. Passion.

I want to be the one out there with him. I want to be the one making him look like that.

Charlie's tongue darts out, wetting his bottom lip.

It's about all I can take. I'm going crazy being here and can't watch this for another minute. Not with the way my thoughts are all jumbled up in my head.

Spinning on my stool, I head out into the cool night air, wishing it was colder. Lights are flickering up and down Main Street. It's like a postcard.

"Brooks. Wait!" Charlie's voice calls from behind me.

"I'm going home, Charlie," I bite back. I don't stop, just stalk down the sidewalk. Finding a lone patch of ice, the boots I'm wearing have me going ass over elbow. Until someone catches me.

"Would you stop?" Charlie huffs, helping to right me. "What's your problem tonight?"

For once, I don't want to talk to him. I don't want to have this conversation.

"My problem?" I turn to face him. His cheeks are pink from dancing and sweat lines his brow.

Why am I noticing these things about him now?

"Yes. You show up at the bar demanding to talk and then leave when I start dancing with someone."

"Because…"

"Because why, Brooks?" Charlie crosses his arms in defense.

"Fuck." I scrub a hand down my face. This isn't how I planned on this night going. On feeling new and different things for Charlie.

My Charlie.

How can watching him dance with one person elicit all these new emotions? Have they always been there, but I never actually let myself feel them?

I need time to think. Time to clear my head to figure out what all this means. Maybe that's what Charlie has been doing all week.

"Hey." Charlie's voice brings me out of my thoughts. "I'm allowed to dance with people, Brooks. So why are you being weird?"

"Me?" I scoff. "You've been avoiding me all week. So who's the one being weird, Charlie?"

"Excuse me for not knowing how to be around you after you learned the truth."

"So ignoring me is the better option?" I ask him.

"Okay, fine. What do you want to know, Brooks?"

Someone bumps into me and it's then I realize we're having this conversation in the middle of the sidewalk with people still out to hear this.

Fuck.

"Do you want to know that I've been in love with you since I realized I was gay? How hard it was to have to hide that all this time because I knew you were straight, only to realize the other night that might not be entirely true?"

"Charlie—"

He doesn't stop. Doesn't take a breath.

"I've buried my feelings for you for years and I was fine with it. Because you were my best friend and I'd rather have you as my friend than not have you at all. But to realize that you might not be straight but that you just aren't into me? It's something I'm trying to come to terms with. It feels like my heart is shattered all over the floor."

The lights play in Charlie's eyes. A Christmas tune is coming from somewhere behind us. My eyes focus on the scar that Charlie got over his lip when he was playing soccer in middle school and fell into the goalpost.

I take a step closer to him, not quite sure what I'm doing. All I know is all common sense has left my head. Because ever since I stepped foot into the Tinsel Tavern tonight, I've been off.

"Brooks." Charlie's voice has gone soft. It's barely a whisper, but it has me closing the distance between the two of us.

The pain here is something I can't take. I can't take the thought of hurting my best friend. But with everything swirling in my head the last week, I act without thinking.

In for a penny, in for a pound, I guess.

I kiss him.

Chapter Ten

CHARLIE

AM I DOING IT WRONG?

Holy shit.

Brooks is kissing me.

Me. *Charlie*.

I'm stunned.

Brooks's lips are warm and sweet, and when his hands cup my cheeks, it shocks me into moving.

"Wait." I push him away. "Wait, stop."

"Am I doing it wrong?" There's a small smile playing at the corner of Brooks's mouth now. So very different from the anger and jealousy I saw there earlier.

"You're…doing it."

"Shit. I'm fucking things up again." Brooks spins on his heel. "Fuck. I keep doing things to fuck up my life and I don't know how to stop."

Brooks and I have been spiraling this week. I know it.

He knows it. It has me fighting a smile because he came to the bar tonight because I was avoiding him.

I didn't know how to be around him after he heard that confession. And now, I just spewed word vomit all over him of everything that I've been feeling this week.

"I should just go," Brooks tells me.

Except I don't want him to. I grab him and lay one on him.

I swallow his shock as he gasps. It takes him a minute to respond, but when his tongue slides against my lips, I react.

Brooks is kissing me back. We're kissing.

Again.

It's even better than the first one as his tongue tangles with mine.

Oh God.

I never wanted to imagine what it would be like to kiss Brooks. It wouldn't have done me or my fantasies any good.

But this? It's better than anything I ever could have hoped to imagine.

When Brooks's warm hands drift lower, pulling me into his chest, I whimper.

It's perfect. Everything from his taste to his warm touch to how his pine scent floods my senses. It's overwhelming in the best way.

I don't know how long we stand outside kissing. I could stand here for the rest of my life and it wouldn't be long enough.

Until Brooks breaks the kiss. I follow his lips, not wanting to let go yet.

"Charlie," he breathes. Brooks drops his forehead to mine.

I press my lips to his and take another kiss. And

another. Before I have to peel myself off him so we don't get arrested for indecent exposure.

"Brooks."

The two of us are standing here, breathing in each other's air. I don't want to say anything. I don't want to break the spell that's fallen over the two of us.

"You know, when I came to the bar tonight, this wasn't exactly what I had in mind."

"Oh yeah? What did you have in mind?" I ask him.

"I just wanted to talk to you. Kissing definitely wasn't on the agenda."

I smirk at him. "Do you want it to be on the agenda?"

Brooks nods against me. "Yes. But I'd prefer it if we maybe didn't do it in the middle of the street."

"I wish I didn't have to go back to work."

"You're not going to go back to dancing with that guy, are you?"

"Why? Were you jealous?"

"I didn't like him touching you," Brooks growls.

I can't hide the smile that spreads across my face. I feel it down to my toes. "You were jealous."

Brooks tries to step out of my hold, but I don't let him get far. "Don't let it go to your head, Charlie."

"I won't be dancing with him. But I do need to get back to the bar."

"When will you be home?" Brooks asks.

"Not until late."

I have never hated the fact that I work late more than I do right this very second. I want to steal Brooks away, hide at my house, and spend all night kissing him.

Learning what he likes and doesn't like. Memorizing the feel of his lips beneath mine.

I want it all.

"I'll see you at home then?"

Brooks takes a few steps back, and the cool air fills the space between us.

"Try to stay awake."

THE SMELL of cinnamon wakes me. Grabbing a sweater, I hop out of bed and follow the sweet scent. The sight that greets me is one I want to remember.

Brooks, standing at my stove, whistling a Christmas tune, and flipping pancakes with Comet at his feet. A tight T-shirt clings to his back.

I've seen Brooks cooking before. This certainly isn't the first time. But something about it feels different. It's quite the sight.

By the time I got home last night, it was almost two. A few regulars were having too good of a time for me to kick them out. Brooks was passed out in his room, and I didn't want to wake him.

"Are you going to stand there and watch me all morning, or do you want some breakfast?"

"Pancakes?" I ask, sitting down on the barstool at the counter, rubbing a hand through my messy hair.

Brooks gives me a warm smile. "Your favorite."

"I could get used to waking up like this."

"To me making you pancakes?"

"To you."

Brooks winks at me before setting down a plate of pancakes in front of me with a steaming mug of coffee.

Black. Just how I like it.

I fight another smile realizing just how much we know about each other. It's the simplest of things, but it has me reaching for the syrup to drown my pancakes so I can stuff my face.

No need to let Brooks see the ridiculous smile there.

I groan. I forgot how good Brooks's pancakes taste. It's been years since I've had them.

"Good?" Brooks peeks over his shoulder at me.

"The fucking best."

I shovel another big bite in my mouth.

"You got home late."

"Sorry." I cut off another bite and take a much smaller piece now. "Some regulars decided to live it up last night."

"Don't be sorry." Brooks comes around the counter with his own plate. Comet is at his feet, no doubt hoping to get a few scraps. "*I'm* sorry I couldn't stay awake."

"It's okay." I spin on the stool to face him as he takes a seat next to me. "How are you feeling?"

"Feeling? About what?"

The smile on his face tells me he knows exactly what I'm talking about. Grabbing his hand so he can't spin away from me, I pull him between my knees. "About last night."

"What happened last night?"

Brooks rests his elbows on the counter and locks eyes with me. It does funny things to my insides. Things that I'm hoping he doesn't regret this morning.

"Do I need to remind you?"

Brooks's smile grows bigger as he moves closer to me and licks his lips. "I would not mind a refresher."

Grasping his neck, I slant my lips over his in the sweetest of kisses. He tastes like coffee and cinnamon, a taste I could get drunk on.

Brooks's tongue darts out to lick my bottom lip and I suck him into my mouth. My mind is swirling over how good it feels to kiss him.

I dig my fingers into the soft strands of hair at the nape of his neck. Licking. Sucking. Drinking my fill of the person I never thought I would get to have.

Until he breaks the kiss.

"Oh yeah. That. I like that."

"Yeah?"

I drop my forehead to his, letting my fingers comb through his hair.

"So much so, that I want to keep doing it."

"You do?" I don't want to hope for too much. I don't know if my heart could take the letdown because Brooks really isn't in the place to be starting something.

"Yeah. I mean, you might have to go slow with me."

"As slow as you need."

Brooks laughs. "I mean, not that slow. I'd like to keep doing the kissing."

"The kissing?" I press my lips to the corner of his mouth. "*Only* the kissing?"

Resting his hands on my thighs, Brooks squeezes them. "I could be down for more."

"Well." I spear a piece of pancake and bite it off my fork. "I guess I better eat my breakfast to get my energy for *more*."

"It is the most important meal of the day," Brooks confirms.

Especially if it leads to more.

Chapter Eleven

CHARLIE

YOU CAN DO BETTER

"We can totally beat you."

"You think so?"

"Yeah. You're old."

"Old? We're not that old."

I watch the argument between Brooks and two teenage boys as we stand at the top of Farmer Dan's hill. Every winter, as soon as the first, thick snow blankets the town, everyone comes out here to go sledding. It's a tradition that goes back as long as I can remember.

If we're really lucky, Dan's wife will occasionally set up a hot chocolate stand at the bottom of the hill to help warm us up. One of the many reasons I love this small town of mine.

That and the fact that Brooks is arguing about who can go faster down a hill right now.

"Okay. You're on." Brooks extends his gloved hand for a quick shake before trudging back over to me.

"What did you get us into?"

Brooks scoffs at me. "They can't just tell us we're old and get away with it."

Glancing behind Brooks, I see the two snickering kids can't be older than thirteen. Then again, all kids looks younger than they probably are. "You realize we're close to two decades older than them?"

"It doesn't mean we're old."

I shift the blue, plastic sled from one hand to the other. "So you challenged them to a sledding contest?"

"Yes," Brooks says matter-of-factly.

"And what happens if they win?"

"I owe them twenty bucks."

"And if you win?"

Brooks smiles at me. "Bragging rights."

I burst out laughing at how ridiculous my best friend is. Even though things might be changing between us, some things will always stay the same. Like the things Brooks ropes me into.

"You ready, sir?" the kid asks as he drops their sled so they can get ready for our competition.

"Sir. I'm not a sir," Brooks mumbles. "C'mon, Charlie. Time to go."

"You know you can take them on by yourself."

Brooks grabs the sled from my hand and drops it down a safe distance from the kids and settles on it. "No, I can't. You're my best friend which means you're here to make sure I don't look like an idiot alone."

"As long as we're in agreement about that."

"That I'm an idiot?"

"Yes."

"You won't be saying that when we beat them." Brooks laughs.

Settling behind Brooks, I scoot in as close as I can. The plastic groans under my added weight as the two of us try to fit onto this tiny sled.

"We can barely fit on this." I shift again, making sure my ass isn't hanging off the back. I don't think Brooks would appreciate that being the reason we lose.

"You mind being close to me?" Brooks turns to look back at me. This close, I can see the playfulness lighting up his hazel eyes. The ends of his auburn hair stick out from under his black hat.

I steal a quick kiss and wrap my arms around his waist. "I don't mind at all."

"On the count of three!" the kids shout from next to us.

"On three, or on 'go' after three?" I ask.

"On three," Brooks and the kids all shout back at once.

"Sorry." I bury my face in Brooks's neck as the countdown is on and wait as Brooks shoves us to a slow start.

"Why aren't we moving?" Brooks huffs, scooting back and forth to try and get the sled to tip over the lip of the hill. The thrust of our hips as we move back and forth has me holding back a groan at the visual.

I can think of more enjoyable things to be doing with our hips than trying to sled.

Leaning back, I push off the ground as we finally gain a bit of traction, but it's useless. The kids are already halfway down the hill by the time we get any momentum.

As the cold wind whips around us, it's hard not to laugh. I can't remember the last time I've come out here to go sledding. With the bar being my main priority, things like this always got pushed to the side.

I would ignore every responsibility if I got to do this with Brooks every day.

Even if we're sliding down the bottom of the hill well after the kids.

"Yes! Told you we'd win!" The kid eggs Brooks on as he hops off his sled and walks over to us. "We're better."

"Yeah, yeah." Brooks reaches into his pocket and pulls out a twenty to hand to the kids. They pump their fists in excitement as they trudge back up the hill.

"I can't believe we lost," I tell Brooks, wiggling off the sled. "I thought for sure our weight would make us go faster."

"I got too cocky, thinking we'd get off faster."

"You want to get off faster?" I waggle my eyebrows at him.

"Charlie!" Brooks looks around to make sure no one is around us. It's busy, but no one is paying us any mind. "You can't say that out here."

"You started it."

"Oh yeah?" Brooks bends down and before I know what happens, a thwack of snow is hitting me square in the shoulder. "What do you have to say about it now?"

"It's on."

Brooks tries to run from me, but I pelt him in the back with my own snowball. He fires one back and it nails me smack on the side of the neck.

"That was low!" I shout after him, scooping up more snow and lobbing it at him. Brooks deftly dodges it.

"You just need better aim." Brooks winks at me.

"It's going to be hard when I'm freezing already."

I can already feel the snow melting, trickling down my neck and soaking the collar of my sweater under my jacket.

"C'mon, Charlie. You can do better," Brooks teases when I throw another ball at him and it misses him again.

Not thinking, I make a move and tackle Brooks to the snow. Grabbing a fist full of snow, I shove it in his face. "How about that?"

"That's not fair!" Brooks sputters. "You're supposed to throw the snow at me."

"And you keep dodging me!"

"Because I'm that good."

Pink blooms over Brooks's cheeks. Ice sticks to his eyebrows as a smile graces his beautiful mouth.

I can't help myself. I lean over him and press a warm kiss to his cold lips. They fit perfectly in mine. Like Brooks's mouth was made for kissing me and only me.

"What was that for?" he whispers, breath hot against my own mouth.

I smile down at him. "Because I can."

"I like that you can."

Brooks pushes off the ground to kiss me again. It's chaste. Nothing like the ones we shared the other night.

There's a buzzing of energy between the two of us. Something that is new and different. This time, when Brooks pulls back, I see the blatant need in his eyes.

It's how I feel around him all the time. I can no longer resist this man.

"You said something about getting off fast?" I nip at his jaw.

"I'd prefer it if we got off slowly."

"Then let's get home fast so we can take it as slow as we want. Preferably several times."

Brooks's answering smile is all I need to light the fire under my ass.

I can't wait to take this slow with him.

Chapter Twelve

CHARLIE

A LOT OF PRACTICE

I don't know if I've ever been so on edge in my life. I like sex. I always have. It was always fun with the guys I dated.

But now, as I'm standing in my room waiting for Brooks to let Comet out, I don't know if I can contain the naked desire that is coursing through me.

Desire for Brooks. Because after years of wanting, yearning for this man, he will finally be in my bed.

The front door closing echoes through the house as I hear Brooks give Comet a bone to keep him busy. The soft sound of his footfalls coming closer to my door amps up my desire even more.

The drive home felt endless. By the time Brooks walks into my room and closes the door, I'm crowding him against it and pressing my lips to his.

Hungry. Hard. Heated.

Fisting Brooks's sweater in my hands, I thrust my leg between his and feel him start to grind down on me.

"Fuck, Charlie."

I nibble my way down his jaw. Brooks's cock is already hard against my leg as I smile into his neck.

Because I'm making him feel that way. *Me.* Charlie.

It's like every star I ever wished upon—where Brooks and I were together in some alternate universe—is exploding and making this happen.

"You like that?"

"Good. So fucking good," Brooks moans.

Tugging Brooks's earlobe between my teeth, I lick the sting away. "There's a lot more where that came from."

Brooks grabs my face and pulls me away, keeping me a mere inch from his sexy face. A face that mirrors everything I'm feeling right now.

"Then show me."

Walking us backward, I spin so I can push Brooks down onto the bed. His tongue darts out, swiping across his lower lip as I take him in.

Brooks Walker is the sexiest man I've ever met. Not wanting to waste a minute of our time together, I grab the hem of his sweater and pull it off him and let it fall to the floor.

A light smattering of hair dusts his chest. His nipples are already hard as I brush a finger over one then the other.

Brooks's abs are rock hard as I sit down on his lap and take his cheeks in my hands to kiss him again.

It's a slow, sensual kiss. Our lips fuse together as our tongues duel for control. My dick is aching in my pants as I slowly rock over Brooks's own hard length.

Brooks's hands start to wander, slipping under the hem

of my T-shirt. The briefest contact there has me throwing my head back as an inferno races through my body.

"Take it off," I beg. I want to feel my skin against his.

Until now, all of our make-out sessions have been tame. I wanted to respect Brooks's need to take it slow. Now, I want to have Brooks buried inside of me.

A sly look comes over his face, then he disappears from view as the fabric covers my eyes before joining his sweater on the floor.

Warm hands drift down my skin. Brooks's eyes stay locked on his hands, as if he can't believe he's touching me like this.

That makes two of us.

Pushing Brooks so he's lying on the bed, I want to be even closer to him. Standing, I make quick work of shedding the rest of my clothes.

"Eager?" Brooks asks from his spot on the bed.

"Very." I nod. No sense in lying. With my dick sticking straight out, there's no hiding how I'm feeling.

I gaze at Brooks as he props up onto his elbows, his hazel eyes raking over my body. Based on the way he licks his lips, I'd say he likes what he sees.

I squeeze my dick to stave off the release I so desperately want with Brooks. It's an ache to have this man inside of me.

I can't take it anymore. Grabbing the hem of his sweats, I take his boxers with them, revealing his thick, just-the-right-length cock.

The biggest surprise? Brooks is uncut.

Fuck. Me.

It's perfect.

"I want to taste you."

I don't give Brooks any more warning than that as I

draw him into my mouth and swallow him down to the base.

"Fuck!" Brooks thrusts up into my mouth as I smile around him. "Charlie. Holy shit."

His dick engulfs my entire mouth as I pull off him and flick the head of his dick that peeks out from the foreskin.

"So good."

I swirl my tongue around the tip of him, then press kisses down one side before licking my way up the other.

"How are you so good at this?" Brooks asks, sinking his fingers into my hair.

"A lot of practice."

Brooks growls. "I don't need to know that."

I pop off him, wiping my mouth. "I'll let you practice on me if you want."

Based on his reaction, Brooks likes that idea.

"I want to."

"Not right now though." I push Brooks back down as he tries to sit up.

"Why not?"

"I like being on my knees too much for you."

In fact, it's my new favorite position as I go back to lavishing his dick with attention.

"I don't want to come down your throat," Brooks tells me.

"You don't?" I ask, sliding off him.

"Not this first time."

"Then I better get prepped."

Getting on the bed, I reach across to my nightstand to grab lube and condoms. But before I can do anything else, Brooks stops me.

"Do we need to use condoms?" he asks.

Brooks is sitting up now with one leg bent on the bed.

Going bare with Brooks? It's almost more than I could

hope for. "My last STI tests were negative, and I'm on PReP."

Brooks nods. "I was negative on my last checkup too. I haven't been with anyone since."

"Soooo…"

Brooks tackles me to the bed. "No condoms then."

When he lies on top of me, I almost come unglued. Finding the lube, I pop it open and coat my fingers.

Brooks rocks back onto his heels to watch as I work myself open. Each prod of my prostate has my dick leaking even more, creating a mess on my stomach.

He grabs my foot and pushes it back, opening me up even more to him. Brooks stares transfixed as I slide two then three fingers inside of myself.

"Do you know how good you look like this?"

"Tell me."

Brooks smiles as he wraps a hand around my cock. His movements are slow, but sure. The friction has my hips thrusting up into his tight fist.

"I like feeling you like this. Seeing how much you want me."

I shake my head. "No. *Need* you."

Brooks rolls his hand over the head of my dick and smooths the wetness down my hard length. "So needy for me, Charlie."

The way he says my name drives me wild. Like he can't believe he's here with me either. That we're actually doing this. I can't wait another minute.

I toss the lube to Brooks. "I'm ready."

Brooks uncaps the bottle and pours probably more than needed onto himself. Slicking his dick, he lies over me and notches himself at my entrance.

Oh God. Even feeling the head there is too much for

me. I have to take several steadying breaths to keep myself from exploding.

Until Brooks slowly pushes past the tight ring of muscle. I dig my fingers into his back, urging him to keep going.

I pull him down to kiss me, adjusting to his size. Loving the feel of him filling me up so perfectly.

"Move."

"You sure?" Brooks asks, whispering against my lips.

I give his ass a light smack. "Yes."

When Brooks pulls out, I lament the loss instantly until he's thrusting back inside. His moves are unsure at first, but when I pull him down to keep kissing me, he gains confidence.

With each jack of his hips, each brush of his cock against my prostate, a heat moves through me that threatens to burn me from the inside out.

As Brooks moves inside me, our kisses are ravaging. The hunger that hangs between the two of us amps up my desire. I don't want to come yet. But Brooks is going faster and faster.

Those hazel eyes of his are full of emotion. It has everything mixing inside of me, like a pop bottle shaken, ready to explode.

I still can't believe this is happening. That this is where Brooks and I are right now. So close to coming together.

"I'm close, Charlie."

"Oh, God. Me too, Brooks," I moan. "I might have an obsession with your cock."

It only takes a few more thrusts before I'm exploding. Cum shoots out of my dick—untouched—as my entire body tightens. It's then I feel Brooks coming inside of me.

Holy hell. I've never felt anything better than this. I've never gone bare with anyone before. Doing it with Brooks?

Fuck. I'm coming undone as he continues unloading inside me before collapsing on top of me.

The two of us stay like this, my skin sticky with sweat and cum as we try to catch our breath.

"Obsessed with my dick, huh?" Brooks says against my chest.

"Oh God. It just slipped out." I start laughing.

"I mean, if you're obsessed, I'll make sure you get your fill."

"Like I am now?"

Brooks shifts, resting his chin on my chest. A happy, soft smile rests on his perfect lips.

"Yes." I brush a piece of hair off his forehead. "How are you feeling otherwise?"

"Good. Great."

I press a kiss to his lips before he goes back to resting on top of me. My fingers drag up and down the notches of his spine.

Right now, everything is perfect. So fucking perfect, it has my heart swelling in my chest.

Except…

I'm wrecked. There is no one else that will ever compare to him.

Brooks has always owned my heart. Now he owns my body too. He's imprinted himself on me in a way that will never be undone.

So much for taking this slow.

Chapter Thirteen

BROOKS

WHATEVER YOU WANT

"Are you okay to do this on your own?"

Charlie shakes his head, holding onto the boards with a death grip. "Please don't leave me."

I skate over to him, kicking snow up on him. "I'm not going anywhere."

"Why did I agree to this?" Charlie mutters.

"The better question is how have you gotten so bad at this?" I ask Charlie. "You used to be so good."

"I can't tell you the last time I went ice skating." Charlie cuts a scathing glare at me.

"Then why'd you want to come?" I skate back a bit from him as he tries to push off from the wall but flails his arms the minute he lets go.

"Because you wanted to come."

I try to hide the smile that blooms on my face. Charlie states this like it's the most obvious thing in the world. It makes me realize just how much he does for me. There was never anything that made Charlie say no to me. No idea too big or too small. He is always in my corner for anything I want to do.

Some days, it makes me wish that I had realized Charlie had feelings for me sooner. Would I be divorced right now? Would Charlie and I be married instead?

I shake the thoughts away. It's not like it would do me any good to think those things right now.

"We don't have to if you don't want to."

Skating up to him, I wrap my arms around him. Light snow is falling around us. The gas lamps are twinkling in the light. The laughs of people around us perforate the air.

Charlie drapes his arms across my shoulders, squeezing tight. More to steady himself, I'm guessing, because his skates start to slide under him.

"No. Wherever you are is where I want to be."

I kiss him. Warm and sweet. I'm learning it's one of my new favorite things. I never knew how much I could like kissing. But with Charlie? I fucking love it. I'm addicted to it.

"I feel like I should do something you want to do when we're done."

"Oh yeah?" There's a glimmer in Charlie's eyes. "Like what?"

I shrug a shoulder and start to skate backward, taking Charlie with me.

"I don't know. I could do with spending more time in bed with you."

A cocky smile spreads across his face. "I think you like that just as much as I do."

"Can't blame a guy."

Charlie screws up his face in thought. "We have ornament painting next week at the tavern."

"I want to do that as much as you do." I smile back at him. "Pick something you want to do, Charlie. Whatever you want to do."

"Okay. I want to decorate you like a sugar cookie and lick the icing off you."

"Sounds good." That thought has my cock stirring in my pants. "As long as I get to lick it off you as well."

"Strip me down and make love to me in front of the fire."

"Are you trying to turn me on right now?"

I shift to try and quell the growing problem in my jeans.

"I want you to fuck me right here on this ice."

"What?" That has me pulling back and looking at Charlie like he's lost his mind.

"Just wanted to see where this 'whatever you want, Charlie' business ends."

I skate back from him, breaking the connection. "I see."

"You can't blame me, can you?"

"Trying to test me, hmm?" I skate another circle around him. "See how much I like you?"

Charlie shakes his head as he stumbles. He reaches out for support and I catch him.

"I already know how much you like me."

"Oh yeah?"

"Yeah."

"And how do you know this?"

"I just do." The grin on Charlie's face is smug. Like he doesn't need to tell me how much I *do* like him.

Because I do. We only just started this thing, but what I'm feeling for Charlie is new and different from anything I've felt before.

I shouldn't be comparing the two, but it's hard not to

when the divorce is still so fresh. Everything with Delia always felt like we had to be on. For people to see just how much we loved each other. It never felt genuine. Like we were always one-upping those around us.

With Charlie? I don't get any of that. We're happy just to be together. Whether it's at home or out doing something together, there's no pressure. Or him letting me do a lap while he's taking a break on the edge of the ice.

It's refreshing. And it has me feeling things I haven't felt in years. Considering where I am in my life, it should scare me. But it doesn't.

"Yeah," I say. "You do."

Leaning against the boards of the rink that sits on the outskirts of town near the Naughty Pine Tree Farm, I skate over to Charlie and rest a hand on either side of him.

"And I know I like you."

I smile back at him, pressing closer to him. "Tell me something I don't know."

"You don't have to be so cocky."

"So sue me; I like knowing how you feel about me."

"I'm beginning to rethink all of this," Charlie tells me, a smirk playing at the corner of his mouth.

"Aren't you the jokester?"

Grabbing his hands, I pull him off the wall and take us on a slow lap of the rink. It's better than the alternative of wanting to devour his mouth.

I find I'm becoming addicted to Charlie. It's easy.

My best friend is probably one of the most genuine people I know. He will go out of his way to help not just me, but anyone. Charlie's big heart is one of the reasons it was easy to say yes to him. To this thing with him.

If it was anyone else, I don't know if I could explore this side of myself. I wouldn't have the courage to do so. To feel safe to do so.

"Stop looking at your feet."

Charlie's eyes snap to mine as I guide us around a group of toddlers using orange cones to help them learn to ice skate.

"It's easier to look down."

"Look at me."

Charlie's deep brown eyes lock onto mine. I loop us around the ice. I can feel Charlie's confidence growing as we keep moving. We're not going fast by any means. The ice is too crowded for that. But as his hands loosen, I let him go and move to skate by his side.

Our shoulders bump as others fly by us, and I grab Charlie's hand to keep him close. As the snow keeps falling, it gets thicker on the ice.

"Should we call it?" I ask Charlie.

"I think so. Maybe we can have some eggnog at home to warm up."

I nod at him and we skate off toward the side through the throngs of people. Finding the bench where we left our boots, I plop down.

"Is it bad my legs are killing me?" Charlie moans as he takes his seat next to me.

"Poor baby. Do you need me to rub you down and make you feel better?"

I press a kiss to his cold cheek.

"No fair. We can't do anything about that now."

"I can take care of you at home."

Charlie rests his head on my shoulder. "I like the sound of that."

The two of us stay like this for I don't know how long, watching the skaters go around the ice. The cool air fills my lungs and a peace settles over me.

I want every day to be like this. With Charlie. Just the two of us and Comet. There's no pressure at all to do or be anything other than who I am. Maybe that's why my marriage ended. I always felt like I had to be someone other than myself.

Not with Charlie.

Charlie accepts me for who I am. He always has.

"Thanks, Charlie," I tell him. Because I don't know if I've ever told him that before.

"For what?" He shifts, resting his chin on my shoulder.

"For being you. For accepting who I am."

"You've always done the same for me."

"Through these last few months, you've been there for me, Charlie. I don't know if I'd be here without you." I press a warm kiss to his lips.

A soft look washes over Charlie's face. One that I see more often than not when he's looking at me. The feelings it stirs up inside me have me questioning a lot of things right now. Things I shouldn't be questioning when we're supposed to be taking this slow.

The way Charlie is looking at me makes me want to throw slow right out the window.

Instead, I do the sensible thing and pull back.

"C'mon. Let's head home and get into our pjs and turn on a Christmas movie."

Charlie grins back at me, as if he's reading my mind. "With a fire?"

"A fire and whatever you want."

"Perfect."

Chapter Fourteen

CHARLIE

BETTER THAN A MOVIE

"Yes, Mom."

Pulling the sweatshirt down over my head, I walk into the living room to find Brooks on the phone.

"I know. Charlie said his parents would be in town next week, so we'll have you over for dinner then."

He smiles at me as I grab a bag of popcorn from the pantry and pop it into the microwave.

"He's good. Really good."

Based on the one side of this conversation I'm getting, I know what they're talking about.

"We're uh, actually, uh…"

What? I think to myself. I want to hear how this sentence is going to end.

"Dating."

I turn around to face him, and the low drone of the

microwave isn't enough to cover up the screams of Brooks's mother.

Spinning on his heel, Brooks has the phone away from his ear with a smile on his face.

A huge smile. One that tells me he's okay with his parents knowing this.

"We can talk more about it later, Mom. I need to go."

I ignore the beep of the microwave and close the distance between the two of us.

"Love you too. Bye."

Wrapping my arms around Brooks's waist, I press a kiss to the side of his neck. "What was that all about?"

"I think you know." Brooks squeezes me back.

"We're dating, huh?"

Forget butterflies. It has lovebirds threatening to burst out of my chest.

"It feels appropriate for what we're doing. Mom will probably grill us with questions, but she is happy. I give it approximately twenty minutes before your mom is calling you to confirm the story."

"Twenty?" I nod, burying my still huge smile into his neck. "You underestimate our moms."

"Well,"—Brooks's warm breath ghosts the shell of my ear—"I told Hunter we were seeing each other too."

I laugh as I break out of his arms to get the popcorn, ignoring the cool air that sweeps in at the loss of him. "And how did that conversation go?"

"He asked me what my intentions were."

I shake my head. Of course he did. The bastard. "What did you tell him?"

"That we're seeing where this goes. Like any new couple."

New. It doesn't feel like it fits us. How long have I known Brooks? Is that his way of already letting me down easy? That this might just be one big experiment for him now that he can do it?

But why would he say that we're dating if it's an experiment? I need to push these thoughts out of my head.

Brooks pulls me out of my spiraling thoughts.

"I can't tell you the last time I stayed in to watch a movie."

"Did you want to go out?" I ask Brooks. "The night's still young. We can."

Brooks shakes his head and drops down onto the couch. With it being a Sunday night, my regular night off, we both opted for a quiet night in. Especially after skating, I didn't want to do anything.

"Nope. I do not want to move from this couch."

Passing a bowl of popcorn over the back of the couch, I grab two mugs of hot cocoa and a bag of peppermint chocolates and take a seat next to Brooks. Comet is spread out on his bed in front of the roaring fireplace, snoring loudly.

"Good." I snuggle up next to Brooks, both of us in plaid pajama pants and sweatshirts. "I'm quite comfortable here."

Brooks presses a kiss into my hair as he wraps an arm around me. I grab the remote and press start on one of the movies we found to watch.

Something about a man going home for Christmas and bringing a fake boyfriend to impress his family.

"Do you think they end up together?" Brooks asks.

I throw a piece of popcorn at him. "Of course they do. Otherwise it wouldn't be a Christmas movie."

"Hey, you never know. What if a farmer from another town comes in and steals his affections and they run off to the big city?"

"Please never write movies."

Brooks shrugs. "I'd watch it."

"Well, shut it, Brooks, so I can watch these two idiots realize their feelings for one another."

Not unlike the two of us, it seems.

As the two men on TV do indeed realize their feelings for each other, it has my thoughts turning to the man whose arms I'm curled up in.

Brooks.

It's still hard to believe that we're together. The last ten days or so have gone by in the blink of an eye. I don't know what the future might hold for the two of us, but it's easy to imagine this being our life.

Curled up on the couch watching movies. Coming home from work and having dinner together. Spending our nights wrapped up in each other in bed.

I snuggle even closer to Brooks.

I want it. It's hard to rein in my feelings for this man now that I finally get to show him what I'm truly feeling.

"Okay, this is pretty cute," Brooks whispers as he reaches across me to grab a piece of the peppermint candy.

"I always like when they realize they're in love." I tilt my mouth up and press a kiss to the underside of Brooks's jaw.

"Mmm. Yeah?"

"Yeah."

"You know what I don't like about these movies?" Brooks asks, shifting on the couch.

"What's that?"

The gaze Brooks shoots in my direction is downright sinful. "Not enough sex."

Sitting up, I throw a leg over Brooks's lap and settle over the growing erection I feel under his soft pants.

"Speaking of sex…there's something I've always wanted to try."

"Oh yeah?" Brooks peppers my face with kisses. "What's that?"

"Docking."

"Docking?" Brooks pulls back, giving me a confused look. "I've never heard of that."

I reach between us, giving his dick a hard stroke. "Well, unless you're uncut, you can't really do it."

"So you're saying I'm perfect for you then?" Brooks waggles his eyebrows at me.

"I'm rethinking everything."

I spin away but he doesn't let me get far. "Tell me what docking is."

"It's basically jacking off, but I pull your foreskin over the head of my dick."

Brooks takes a minute to think about it. "Like you're pulling into a dock."

I nod. "That's it."

Brooks pushes me off him and stands, linking our hands and leading us back toward my bedroom.

Shutting the door behind us, Brooks throws me against it and swoops in, kissing me like he's never kissed me before.

It's like Brooks is claiming me as his own with each stroke of his tongue against mine. My dick is aching in my pants to escape, and I can't help myself when I thrust my hips toward Brooks, meeting his own equally hard dick.

"Get naked."

Brooks walks back toward the bed, throwing off his sweatshirt before kicking off his pajama pants. The more skin he reveals, the harder I get. Shoving my hand into my own pants, I give myself a long, slow pull to stave off my release.

"Are you going to get naked with me?" Brooks asks as he lies back on the bed, throwing off his boxers.

Pulling off my sweatshirt, I stalk toward the bed, taking in the hunk of a man now lying on the soft duvet. His leaking dick is making a mess on his stomach. Leaning over him, I swipe my tongue through his pre-cum. Fuck, I love the salty taste of him.

"Do you know how good you taste?"

"Show me."

The lascivious smile he gives me hits me right in the chest. My heart pounds as I lick a path through the pre-cum on his stomach, swiping at his nipple as I make my way up to his mouth. I commit him to memory. His taste. The feel of his hard chest beneath my fingertips as he writhes with want.

His groan travels right to the part of me that always wanted my best friend. The part that is excited and scared because what if this is all we'll have. Memories of Christmas nights together on the couch before we move on from one another.

Brooks's lips seek mine out in a greedy way and I let him devour me, his taste still on my tongue. I never thought I would love kissing him as much as I do. It's intense. Fiery. Raw in a way I've never experienced.

"I taste even better on your lips, Charlie."

"So fucking good, Brooks." I pepper his mouth with kisses as I take off my pants and grind down on him. "I need you."

It's the truest words I've ever spoken. I need Brooks something fierce.

"Explain this to me."

"Let me show you instead."

I want my hands on his hard length. Reaching over to the nightstand, I grab the lube and slick both of us up.

"Hold yourself open like this."

Opening the foreskin, I let Brooks hold it open as I stretch my own foreskin and line the two of us up. Guiding my skin, I envelop his cockhead before releasing it and pulling his skin over both of us, suctioning us together.

"Fuck. This feels amazing," Brooks hisses.

"So damn good, Brooks."

This is something I've never done. I've always wanted to try it, but never had a partner who wanted to do it with me. Would I have wanted to try it with someone? Would I have trusted them enough to do it?

Sure, it's sex, but it feels more intimate. Doing it with Brooks for the first time? It has my heart banging around in my chest as I wrap a hand around our connected dicks.

It feels bigger doing it with the man I'm in love with.

"Why did you not suggest this before?" Brooks clasps his other hand around my neck and pulls me close. His breath is hot on my mouth. "I want to do this all the time now."

I squeeze harder as I reach the base of his cock. "I think I can make that happen."

"You better," he groans. "Faster."

"Oh no." I smile at him. "I don't want this to end."

"I'm so close, Charlie. C'mon. Make me come."

Brooks tries to make me go faster, but I don't. I love the slow, methodical movement of my hand. This feeling is so incredible, I don't want it to end. Being this close and connected to Brooks is something I never thought I'd ever get to experience.

And it's that thought that has me starting to move faster.

"Yessss," he hisses. "That's it, Charlie. Are you going to come for me? Do I get to taste you this time?"

"Fuck!" I shout as I start to come. It's wet and tight and

the explosion of lust and desire I'm feeling is something I've never experienced before.

"Yes!" Brooks mirrors my own release, throwing his head back. Cum is leaking out between where we're connected. His? Mine? I don't know, but the sight of it has me pulsing again.

And watching as Brooks swipes his fingers through our cum and brings them to his lips?

Fuck. Me.

I take a lazy kiss from him, tasting our release on his mouth.

"Oh yeah," I moan, licking my lips. "We need to do this again."

"Yes, we do," Brooks agrees.

Forever, if I have anything to say about it.

Chapter Fifteen

SO MUCH FOR A MERRY CHRISTMAS

"Dinner smells good."

"Thanks."

Brooks leans back, waiting for a kiss, which I happily give. It's not a Christmas dinner, but it might as well be.

Brooks, ever the chef, prepared beef Wellington, Brussels sprouts, green beans, and fresh cranberry sauce. Bacon-wrapped dates are sitting out as an appetizer. My contribution? I bought rolls from the local bakery on my way home.

"Now if only everyone would hurry up and get here so we can eat, they can go home and we can have dessert."

"What's this dessert you're thinking of?" Brooks asks.

I slide my hands under his apron, resting just above his belt. "You."

"Not the chocolate mousse I made everyone?"

I press a kiss into his neck. "Maybe licking it off you."

"Charlie," Brooks moans. "You cannot do this to me five minutes before our families come over for dinner."

"Why not?" I nip at his ear. I know we don't have time to fool around. But it doesn't mean I'm not going to edge this man as much as possible.

It's hard to believe how fast time has flown by since we started this, spending every spare minute we can together.

It's about as perfect a holiday as I ever could have hoped for.

Brooks sidesteps me to reach for a jar of spices next to the oven. "You're going to get us in trouble, Charlie."

"Sue me. I can't help it if you're irresistible."

Brooks winks at me. "Get the drinks out. They'll be here any minute."

It's as if his words summon them. A knock echoes at the front door followed by Comet's barks.

Comet follows me to the door, his tail wagging wildly as it swings open and he bolts for Brooks's parents. My own parents smile down at the happy guy, waiting patiently for their turn to love on the exuberant furball.

"Charlie!" Mom wraps me in a hug, shaking snow off her coat. "I've missed you. I can't believe I had to hear from Jane that you and Brooks are dating. No phone call? Nothing. It's like I don't even exist."

"That's a touch dramatic."

Dad pats me on the shoulder as he walks in with Brooks's parents behind him. "You know she wishes you lived closer so she could hear everything that's going on in your life."

"You're the ones that moved, not me."

"We don't see you enough," Mike, Brooks's dad, tells me as he takes off his coat and bends over to pet Comet.

"I spend most of my time at the bar," I tell him.

"Not all your time." Brooks comes up and hugs his parents and mine. "I get plenty of his time too."

I steal a kiss from Brooks.

My mom claps her hands together. "Jane, aren't they just so cute? Who would have ever thought they'd be together?"

"Certainly not me," Jane answers. "I love it."

Brooks rolls his eyes as he heads back into the kitchen to get eggnog ready for everyone. "Okay, Mom. Come grab a drink. Dinner is ready."

Brooks sets the Beef Wellington in the center of the table as everyone takes their seats with a glass of eggnog in hand.

"Brooks, you've outdone yourself," Dad says. "You should be a chef."

Brooks smiles at him and passes a dish to him. "I'm having too much fun working for Hunter."

"Really? Out at the tree farm?" Mom asks.

Brooks nods and takes a helping of green beans onto his plate. "I started helping him with his website. He's got some great ideas. I'm really liking it."

"You're good at what you do." Jane pats Brooks on the arm.

Conversation is light as everyone piles their plates high with food and digs in. Every bite is delicious. The perfect dinner with the best company.

After all the dinner dishes are cleared, I grab the dessert and bring it out for everyone.

"You've outdone yourself, Brooks," I tell him as I spoon a bite of the chocolatey dessert into my mouth.

"We might have to move home just to have you cook for us," Mom says.

"I don't know if even that's a big enough draw to get her home in the winter," Dad says. "But it's tempting."

I wave them off. "You love the sunshine too much to move back."

"Maybe we need to move down there. Now that Brooks doesn't need us," Jane says.

"Really?" Brooks asks, dropping his spoon down onto his plate. "You want to move to Florida?"

Mike shrugs a shoulder. "We've thought about it. We didn't want to leave when you were going through everything. But now?"

"Now we're not as worried about you." Brooks's mom smiles at the two of us. "It's so nice to see you doing so well after the divorce, sweetheart."

"Thanks, Mom," Brooks tells her. "All Charlie."

Brooks leans over and gives me a sweet kiss. Hearing his words has a warmth spreading through me. I would do this again in a heartbeat to see Brooks this happy.

"Aww, Nancy. Do you think we can start planning their wedding now?" Brooks's mom asks my mom.

"You've always imagined a Christmas wedding, haven't you, Charlie?" Mom asks.

"Mom. Brooks just got divorced."

"Besides," Brooks interjects, "I have no plans on getting married again. Problem solved."

"What, really?" Jane asks. "You don't want to get married again?"

Brooks shakes his head at his mom. "Is this something we really need to be talking about right now?"

"I'm just surprised, that's all."

"Really?" Brooks asks. "I don't think it's that surprising considering I just got divorced."

"But Charlie." Jane turns her attention to me. "You want to get married, right?"

"I mean, I always planned on it."

The only problem was that I never found someone I

wanted to get married to. Now I have Brooks. Who is adamant about not getting married again.

Brooks pins me with a pleading look, wanting to explain himself. But why would he?

Logically, I knew this. But I don't think I ever let myself comprehend it.

Eggnog curdles in my stomach. Do Brooks and I have an end date? Whenever I pictured the two of us together, that was it. When Brooks fell in love with me, we'd be together forever. We rushed into this, and I never really stopped to think about what would happen if it didn't work out. I never thought that our feelings toward marriage would get in the way.

Could I handle never getting married? I've always wanted it, ever since I was a little boy. To show the world that I love this man so much, that we're tied together forever.

"Listen." Jane stands, collecting the dessert dishes from the table. "We're going to head home. Nancy, Bill, would you like to come over for a drink?"

"Sure."

They say goodbye quickly while I head to the sink to start doing the dishes. How did it go from having an enjoyable evening with everyone to this weird limbo? To worrying about what our future holds.

"Hey." Brooks comes up next to me and grabs the sponge from my hand. "Can we talk?"

"Sure."

I don't look at him, staring at the bubbles in the sink.

"Look, Charlie. I don't want to lie to you. Getting married isn't in the cards for me. My marriage ended in disaster. Hell, I'm staying at your house because I still don't have a place to live."

"I know."

"Do you?" Brooks grasps my chin and turns my gaze to meet his. There's a sadness in his eyes.

"Yeah."

Maybe. Maybe I've been lying to myself this whole time. Maybe Hunter was right. Not that I'll ever admit that to him, but God, this feeling sucks right now.

"Charlie."

"I'm going to go to bed." I step out of Brooks's hold. "I need to do inventory tomorrow at the bar, so it's going to be a long day."

"Okay."

It looks like Brooks wants to say more, but he doesn't. What could he say to make me feel better? He never lied to me.

Turns out I was just lying to myself.

So much for a merry Christmas.

Chapter Sixteen

BROOKS

A LITTLE SPEED BUMP

"Charlie. Are you ready to go?"

Pulling a sweatshirt over my head, I jog down the stairs to see Charlie laid out on the couch with a mug in his hand.

"I think I'm going to skip it tonight."

"You don't want to go paint ornaments together? It's your night."

I'm shocked. I know this is Charlie's favorite night at the Tinsel Tavern. He loves that he can do something fun and at the same time raise money to help others that are down on their luck during the holidays.

Fuck.

Everything between the two of us is all muddled up.

Not being up for this? Charlie is up for everything all the time.

I've royally fucked this up.

We're together, but not. I know Charlie is putting on a happy face for me, and I hate it. I hate that I can tell he's miserable. Whenever I ask, he tells me he's fine.

I hate that word. *Fine.*

He's so not *fine.*

"The guys can run it without me."

"I can stay home with you."

"No." Charlie shakes his head, now looking at me. "I want you to go."

"Are you sure?" Comet brushes by me and hops onto the couch.

"I'm sure. Didn't you say you needed to talk to Hunter anyway?"

"That can wait until later."

"No. You go. Have fun."

I hate the sadness clinging to Charlie. It's a living, breathing thing that's hanging between the two of us.

I don't want to leave. I want to stay here with Charlie and convince him to talk to me. But I don't think that's going to happen tonight.

"Okay."

Charlie grabs the remote and flips to another channel and settles back onto the couch.

"Tell the guys hi for me." He doesn't look at me.

"I'll be home later."

"See you then."

I broke my best friend and I'm not quite sure how to fix him.

"WHERE'S CHARLIE TONIGHT?" Hunter asks, dipping his paintbrush into the blue paint.

"He's at home."

"Why?" Ollie asks, not looking at me but focusing on his own snowman ornament. "He loves ornament night."

I shrug. "He didn't feel like coming out."

Hunter sets his paintbrush down and pushes back into his seat. "What'd you do?"

"Excuse me?" I pierce him with a hard stare. "What did *I* do? Why do you assume I did something?"

"Charlie's not here on one of his favorite nights of the year. I'm only assuming you did something to make him stay home."

"I told him I didn't want to get married again."

This draws Ollie's attention. "Charlie knew that."

"I—"

"I don't think he really thought about it before they started hooking up," Hunter interrupts.

"That." I point at Hunter. "Charlie has always wanted to get married and I don't."

"Ahh." Ollie adjusts his glasses and sets his paintbrush down. "Now he doesn't want to force you into staying because you're on two different paths."

Even the thought of losing him now is too much to bear. It's *Charlie*. The one person in my life I can always count on. Who's always been there for me.

I…

"I love him."

"We know." Ollie has a duh look on his face.

"No, I mean I'm in love with him."

Hunter is smiling at my confession. "Took ya long enough to get there."

I roll my eyes at him. "I've always loved him, but it's different now."

Hunter and Ollie exchange a look. "What's—"

"So you love him." Hunter is quick to interject, changing the subject.

"Yes. He's the best person I know and I don't want to lose him. But I don't know how to keep him."

"Have you tried telling that to him?" Ollie asks.

I voice my biggest fear to these two. "But what if he doesn't want to stay in a relationship with me? What if he can't get past the whole not getting married thing?"

Hunter drops his paintbrush and looks at me. If I weren't used to him by now, I'd cower under his stare.

"You know what I know about Charlie?" Hunter asks.

"What?"

"It's not so much the marriage, but the tying two lives together."

"Isn't that marriage?" Ollie asks.

Hunter smiles at him before continuing. "It doesn't have to be. Charlie wants someone to commit to him. To show the world that you two belong to one another. Charlie wants that more than anything."

"How do you know that?"

And why do I not know this about my best friend.

"Read between the lines, Brooks."

My gaze flicks to Ollie's before settling back on Hunter. "Didn't you need to talk to me about the website?" Hunter asks, changing the subject.

"Oh. Yeah." I forgot about that. "Can we maybe do it on Monday?"

"Sure. We can talk about some long-term ideas I have then."

"Really?" I ask. "I thought you only needed me for the website revamp."

Hunter nods. "I did. But you did a great job. Your ideas are good and I could use someone like you."

"Wow. Just like that?"

"Just like that."

"Even if Charlie and I break up?"

Hunter shakes his head. "You won't."

"You're pretty confident about that."

"I've seen the two of you together. This is a little speed bump."

Staring down at my half-painted ornament, an idea starts to take shape. I have no idea if it will work, but it's worth a shot.

If it means I get to keep Charlie, I'll do anything.

Chapter Seventeen

CHARLIE

I LOVE YOU SNOW MUCH

Christmas Eve eve.

I should be more excited than I am, but I'm not. Turning over in bed, I'm met with an empty space. It's cold to the touch.

I guess I should get used to this.

Sighing, I turn back over and stare out the windows. Gray clouds are clinging to everything. It's not snowing, but it's supposed to dump over a foot of snow later. Thank God the Tinsel Tavern is closed until after Christmas.

I exhale. I need to not let this ruin the holiday. Brooks has been happy. Happier than I've seen him in ages. I need to put him first.

If only the thought of that didn't break my own heart.

I flop onto my back as Christmas music starts to filter into my room from the living room.

The bedroom door opens and the clatter of paws on

the hardwood floor is my only warning before Comet jumps onto the bed. He attacks my face with morning kisses.

"Hi, buddy."

I rub his head as his owner follows him into the room.

"Breakfast?" Brooks asks, carrying a tray. There's a plate of donuts and two mugs of coffee.

"When did you get donuts?" I sit up, resting against the headboard.

"I've been up for an hour. Comet and I have already been into town and gone on our walk."

"You have a lot of energy."

"Because I'm excited." There's a hesitant smile on his face.

"For what?" I grab a red-frosted donut with candy cane sprinkles and take a hearty bite.

"For this." Brooks sets a small brown box with a green ribbon on the tray.

"What is it?"

"Open it and find out." Brooks scoots it closer as Comet huffs, as if telling me I'm an idiot for even asking.

I roll my eyes at him. "Christmas isn't for two more days."

"So?" Brooks shrugs a shoulder. "Who says you can't open a gift before then?"

Grabbing the small box off the tray, I pull the ribbon apart and take the lid off. It's a snowflake ornament. One that looks hastily painted.

The words "I love you snow much" are painted across the front in a silver color that glitters.

"What is this?" I look at Brooks with confusion. "Did you make this the other night?"

He nods. "I did."

"And?"

"I don't think the message is sinking in yet," Brooks tells me.

"What? I love you snow much? What's that supposed to mean?"

Brooks laughs. "It means I love you."

"But…"

Brooks takes the tray and sets it on the nightstand before taking my hand in his. The ornament sits between the two of us.

"Charlie, I love you. This thing between us took me by surprise. I never expected it when I moved in here. But I wouldn't change a thing. I want to be with you. And I know we're on two different pages about marriage, but it doesn't mean I don't want the world to know that you're mine and I'm yours."

"Yeah?" Tears sting my eyes.

Brooks squeezes my hand. "Yeah. If you need me to wear a T-shirt every single day that says 'Property of Charlie Palmer,' I'd do it. Because I love you and I'm yours."

An undignified snort leaves me as tears start to roll down my cheeks. "You're not just saying this? Because that'd be really mean. All I want is to be yours, and if it means not getting married, I can come to terms with that."

"I'm not just saying this. I have no plans of going anywhere. It's you and me, Charlie. You and I can write the rules on what we want our life to be. As long as we're together."

I look down at the ornament in my lap. I give a watery laugh. "I love you snow much too, Brooks."

Brooks smiles, wide and happy, as he grasps the back of my neck and pulls me in close.

"Not as much as I love you."

He seals his lips over mine and it's about the best kiss of my life.

"I can't believe you made me this."

Brooks shrugs a shoulder. "I'll have to do better next time. I was on a crunch to get it done and it was all I could think of."

I shake my head. "It's perfect. Absolutely perfect."

"Hunter gave me a lot of shit for it."

"Of course he did."

"I knew you'd love it."

I nod. "It is going to get a place of honor on the tree. Front and center."

"Perfect."

Brooks throws one leg over my lap and settles on top of me. The soft fabric of his shirt brushes against my bare chest as he closes his mouth over mine.

It's a promise. The promise of a future together. It might not be what I always imagined my life looking like, but ever since Brooks and I started this thing, it's been so much more.

I never thought I'd get to be with him. So what if we don't get married? I'm still getting my best friend in a way I only dreamed about.

We're together. That's all I need.

I break the kiss, resting my forehead against his as we breathe each other in.

"You're my best friend, Charlie," Brooks whispers. "I love you in so many ways, it's hard to count."

"I love you, Brooks. As long as I have you, I'll have everything I need." Comet gives a bark. "Okay, you too, Comet."

The dog in question stretches out along my legs, making himself comfortable.

"I don't think I'd ever be able to leave because Comet might love you the most," Brooks tells me.

"That's a given." I laugh.

Brooks wraps his arms around my shoulders and pulls me in for a hug, burying his face in my neck. "I'm sorry it took me so long to catch up to you."

"I'm just glad you did."

If this is what I get with Brooks, I would've waited a lifetime for even one minute with him.

Because waiting for Brooks was worth it.

Epilogue

YOU MADE ME AN ORNAMENT?

Breathe, Brooks. Breathe.

Everything about this night has gone off without a hitch. Two of our best friends are getting married, and tonight has been the perfect night.

Dinner. Dancing. Drinks. I know that this marriage is going to last. I have no doubts that these two will make it.

Watching these two fall in love and plan their wedding has restored my faith in the institution. Not that falling in love with Charlie hasn't, but I had to separate him from marriage.

Because otherwise, I wouldn't be freaking out between the pine trees right now.

"What are you doing out here?" Charlie comes outside, tugging his jacket on over his dark purple suit jacket.

I hate that he's hiding in the oversize winter coat. When he walked out of our room earlier, it took every ounce of restraint I had not to push him back into bed and have my way with him.

But I'll get that tonight.

"Needed some air."

"Brooks, it's freezing out here." Charlie throws my own coat over my shoulders and pulls me toward him.

Just like Charlie. Always taking care of me. It has a smile tugging up the corner of my mouth.

"What's that face for?" Not even two minutes outside and pink blooms on Charlie's cheeks. The tip of his nose is red.

"Can't I just appreciate my boyfriend?"

A smile lights up Charlie's face. Every time he looks at me, I see this same face. I don't know how I never saw it before. Because he looks at me with so much love, I don't know how I deserve it.

"You can always appreciate me. But can't we do it inside?" Charlie whines. "My toes are going to freeze off."

"C'mere." Linking hands with Charlie, I drag him between the rows of Christmas trees. These trees weren't cut down this year. Hunter told me all about how he does it, but right now, that doesn't matter.

I want a moment with Charlie. A moment I've been dying to have with him all night.

"Seriously, Brooks. I'm freezing."

I smile back at him, drawing him into my arms. "Then how about I warm you up?"

His lips are cool as I capture them with mine. Mmm. I don't think I'll ever get used to this.

The way my stomach flutters when my lips touch his. The soft moans he makes as my tongue sweeps into his mouth. His hands fisting under my coat to keep me close.

The smell of pine is strong as we kiss. And kiss. And

kiss. If only it weren't so damn cold, I'd drop to my knees right here and show him just how much I want him.

How much I'll always want him.

I pull back, but Charlie stops me. "No. Another minute."

"Aren't you cold?" I whisper against his lips between small pecks. He tastes like the champagne cocktail he's been sipping on all night.

"Not with you."

Wind sweeps through the farm, rustling the pine trees. Charlie's brown hair blows into his eyes. His eyes hold so much adoration for me, I know what I'm about to do will only scratch the surface.

The love I have for Charlie runs deep, so etched into me, that I don't know how it can continue to grow, but it does. It's a part of me. Knowing what he does for me every day is something I don't know if I'll ever be able to repay to him.

But it makes me want to. In a way I never thought I'd be able to do for him. Something I can thank Hunter for helping me through.

"Marry me."

Charlie steps back. "Excuse me?"

"You heard me."

"Oh, I heard you alright. But marry you?"

I scoff. "Why do you sound so against the idea?"

"Because, and I quote, 'I will never get married again, even if the world is on fire and it would save humanity.'"

I rub my hands together, trying to warm my fingers. "I did say that, didn't I?"

"You had some pretty choice words on marriage."

"Hey, can you blame me? It was night one as a single man."

That pulls a smile from Charlie's face. "I remember. Because a short while later you and I got together."

I drop my forehead to his. "Probably the best decision I ever made."

Charlie presses a quick kiss to my lips. "Which is why I won't make you marry me."

"But what if I did change my mind?"

"You're changing your mind on marriage?" Charlie sounds skeptical and I can't blame him.

It's cold. The snow is starting to seep into the hems of my pants and soak my socks. Doing this out here might not have been my best idea. "I changed my mind on you, didn't I?"

"You did."

"And I changed my mind on marriage."

Charlie's fingers dig into my back, keeping me close. "But why? I know you agreed to think about it, but I've kind of come to terms with being with you like this."

"And that's why I want to marry you." I cup his cheeks. They've pinked up even more since we've been kissing. I love that I can bring this out in him. "I want everyone to know that I belong to you, Charlie. That you're mine."

"Yeah?" His eyes glaze over.

"Shit. I'm doing this all wrong."

Stepping back, I grab one of Charlie's hands and sink to one knee.

"You're going to get wet." Charlie's voice is watery.

"I don't care. I love you, Charlie. More than I ever thought possible. I never knew this was a kind of love that I could have. It shocks me every day that you chose me. That you love me and that I, for some lucky reason, get to love you back."

"I think I'm the lucky one," Charlie tells me, tears rolling down his cheeks.

"Marry me, Charlie. Marry me and let's spend the rest of our lives being lucky together."

Charlie stares at me before bursting out into laughter. "Oh my God. Could you be any more cheesy?"

I stand, getting cold now from kneeling. "Ouch. This is how my proposal is met? I'm rethinking the entire thing. I even had an ornament painted at home to commemorate the occasion."

Charlie's face goes soft. "How can I say no when you made me an ornament?"

"That's what gets you to say yes?" I scoff. "I should have brought it with me. Lead with that."

"Well, then it's a good thing you made it because I'm saying yes to you."

"Me and my ornament?"

Charlie waggles his eyebrows. "That sounds dirty."

I laugh, loving this man. "Of all the ways I imagined this going, this is not how I pictured it."

Charlie throws his arms over my shoulders. "Did you imagine me falling all over you and jumping into your arms and confessing my love to you?"

"I mean, yeah. A little more emotion wouldn't hurt."

I act hurt, but I'm not. Because I didn't miss the yes in between all of this. It's why I'm not prepared when Charlie throws himself at me.

Wrapping his legs around me, he knocks us both over into the snow as he peppers my face with kisses.

"Of course I'll marry you, you idiot!" Charlie shouts between bursts of laughter. "I love you so much, Brooks. I don't know if it's because you proposed or it's the cold, but I'm in shock!"

Pressing one last kiss to Charlie's lips, I pull back. "It's time to get you inside then. I don't want my fiancé to catch frostbite."

"What a thoughtful fiancé *I* have."

Charlie is beaming as we both stand. Reaching into my pocket, I pull out the small velvet pouch and find the ring in there.

It's a titanium steel band—something that will hold up on the long nights at the tavern.

"It's perfect." Charlie catches my hand as I slide the ring onto his finger. It's a bit snug, but he forces it down.

"I love you, Charlie."

"I love you, Brooks."

Linking hands with him, I lead us toward the barn where the music is blasting and the reception is still in full swing. With midnight closing in, there will surely be fireworks to celebrate their wedding and the new year.

Everything about this night is perfect. Charlie on my arm. Celebrating our friends.

I never thought I would get this lucky again. Who knew all it would take was opening my eyes to see what was right in front of me?

My Charlie.

My best friend.

The love of my life.

My fiancé.

I never thought Christmas could get better than this.

Looking over at Charlie as the warmth of the barn hits us, I realize just how wrong I was.

And I've never been happier.

THE END

Want to see how Brooks and Charlie spend their first Christmas together? Keep reading for a bonus scene now!

Want more bi-awakening stories? Check out Best of Both
Worlds today!

123

BROOKS

"I think we need to up our game," I tell Charlie. "This house might be too much."

Charlie pulls Comet to a stop at the house at the end of the street. Every inch of the yard is filled with inflatables. Lights are strung on every surface on the exterior, and the lights from inside are just as bright.

"I didn't realize there was a limit to your love of Christmas." I laugh.

Comet lets out a bark at one of the oversized reindeers as it sways in the wind.

"See?" Charlie points at the dog in question. "Even Comet thinks it's too much."

I reach down and pat his head before taking the leash from Charlie as we continue our stroll up the road.

"Okay, now I love this house," Charlie tells me, sipping on his hot chocolate. "Definitely my favorite."

I pull Comet to a stop in front of the house at the end of the block. "Of course the house with rainbows is your favorite."

"Hey." Charlie swats at me with a gloved hand. "You

need to learn to love them now. Besides, they're fun and happy."

An inflatable rainbow sits on the roof of the house. Colorful lights are strung along the columns on the wraparound porch.

"You're my bright little rainbow, Charlie." Leaning over, I drop a peck on Charlie's cold cheek. "I don't need any more rainbows than that."

"So cheesy, Brooks. Is this what I have to look forward to for the rest of our lives?"

I grab Charlie's hot chocolate and take my own sip before guiding us along the sidewalk. "I've always been this cheesy. You love it."

"I don't know why."

Linking my arm through his, a sense of contentment washes over me. Being here with Charlie after having spent our first holiday together as a couple.

We had our families over for Christmas lunch after a lazy morning curled up in front of the fire.

It was perfect. Everything about today has been perfect.

A cold wind sweeps down the road as we pass house after house, lit up in the darkness. Some have blowup Santa's decorating the front yard while others have candy canes lining the sidewalk. It's a chaotic mix.

"I'm ready to head home. It's getting cold," I tell Charlie.

Comet barks in agreement in front of us and turns toward the house, picking up the pace.

"I can think of one way to warm you up."

"Does it involve more of that?" Charlie nods to the mug in my hand.

A sly smile spreads across my face. "It does not."

"Care to show me?"

"OH FUCK, BROOKS," Charlie groans.

I hum around him, bobbing up and down as I suck on his dick. My form still isn't great, but from the way Charlie is squeezing my hair in his hand, he doesn't care. I smile around him, before pulling off completely.

"I like seeing you like this."

Pushing both of his legs up, I drag a finger around his balls and love the sound of his moans. The way his body shudders.

"Are you trying to drive me crazy, Brooks?"

Charlie pops up onto his elbows to stare down at me. There is nothing but love in his eyes. Well, love and frustration.

"Doesn't it make it better when I get you on edge like this?"

I press a kiss to his thigh. Nibble on the tender skin there. Fuck. His skin is so damn soft that it has me grinding down into the bed. My own cock is aching. I want to bury myself inside this man, but not until I suck him off.

"If I say yes, will you hurry up?"

"Toss me the lube."

Because if Charlie is going to come, I'm going to be coming inside his tight little ass as soon as he does.

"Fuck. Yes."

Charlie leans across the bed to grab the lube from the nightstand and tosses it to me. I waste no time slicking my fingers and pushing one inside of him. He widens his legs to take me deeper. I know the minute I peg his prostate because he lets out a low, sensuous growl.

"Do you know how hot it is to see you taking my finger like this? Sexiest thing ever."

"Feels even better. Keep doing that."

Charlie's head is thrown back in pleasure, his eyes squeezed shut.

Smiling to myself, I do as instructed. My moves are slow and measured as I add a second finger before swallowing Charlie's dick to the back of my mouth. My moves get sloppier as I add a third finger, stretching him.

"I'm coming. Fuck, Brooks! Fuck!" Charlie shouts, pushing off the bed and shoving his cock deeper down my throat. I choke around him but don't let go. I love the salty taste of his cum as it slides down my throat.

"Holy shit. That was incredible," Charlie breathes out.

I pop off of him. "Don't get too comfortable."

Before he can say anything else, I line my own hard dick up with his hole and push inside. We're both sticky with sweat as I cover his body with mine.

It's unreal getting to be with Charlie like this. Seeing his pleasure written on his face is a high I've never experienced.

Charlie links his hands behind my neck and pulls me in for a kiss. Our tongues tangle as my hips thrust in and out of Charlie's tight ass.

"Are you going to come in my ass?" Charlie whispers against my lips.

"Fuck." I tug his bottom lip between my teeth before jacking my hips once, twice then exploding inside him.

Charlie's warm hands hold me close as I continue pumping my hips. Heat rolls through me as I see stars.

"So fucking good." I puncture each word with a kiss to his neck before collapsing on top of him.

We're both a sweaty mess, but I don't move. I want to stay in Charlie's arms for as long as possible.

Forever, even.

"How does it keep getting better?" Charlie traces each notch in my spine. "It shouldn't be this good."

"Just you wait…" I'm breathless.

"For what?"

"Until I get really good at knowing what you like."

A rumble of laughter vibrates through me. "So you're saying this isn't your A game?"

I rest my chin on Charlie's chest and stare up at him. "I'm still learning. I have a lot for you to teach me."

Charlie rolls his eyes at me. "What a chore that will be."

Sliding out of him, I lie down next to him. "Maybe that can be your present to me."

Flipping us so he's hovering over me, there's a playful look on Charlie's face. "You want me to be your sex tutor?"

I burst out laughing. "Is that what we're going to call it?"

"Do you have a better way to describe it?"

I shake my head. "I like sex tutor."

"Good." Charlie presses a quick kiss to the corner of my mouth. "Then get ready for your present."

Best. Present. Ever.

Acknowledgments

BOOK TWENTY-THREE IS OUT IN THE WORLD!

There's always an idea behind a story. Some hit me like lightning in the middle of the night while others come from real life. My oldest friend, Russ, and I were at a wedding and we both thought the best man's speech was a love confession (spoiler alert: it wasn't). But after a few too many drinks at the open bar and a shared Uber ride home, he asked me "Is this a romance novel?" To which I already had the entire plot of Merry In Moose Falls in my head. I spent the next day making notes and plotting and knew this would be my first holiday novella. I love my two goobers and hope you did too!

I'm going to keep this one short and sweet. Thank you to Tina, my author friends, and all of the amazing readers for sharing your love for my books. I can't wait to see what this next year will bring!

Happy holidays!
<3 Emily

Sideline Infraction

Illegal Contact

The Big Game

Moose Falls, Maine

Merry in Moose Falls

A Grump in Moose Falls

Standalones

Off the Deep End

The Highland Escape

Power Pose

Love Pucked - a sapphic hockey romance, coming late 2025

The Ainsworth Royals

Royal Reckoning

Reckless Royal

Royal Relations

Royal Roots

The Love Abroad Series

An Icy Infatuation

A French Fling

A Sydney Surprise

Scan the QR code to read my books now!

About the Author

After winning a Young Author's Award in second grade, Emily Silver was destined to be a writer. She loves writing inclusive stories, with strong heroines and the swoony men who fall for them.

A lover of all things romance, Emily started writing books set in her favorite places around the world. As an avid traveler, she's been to all seven continents and sailed around the globe.

When she's not writing, Emily can be found sipping cocktails on her porch, reading all the romance she can get her hands on and planning her next big adventure!

Find her on social media to stay up to date on all her adventures and upcoming releases!